Someone Waiting

Other Large Print books by Anne Maybury
in Thorndike Large Print:

Green Fire

Someone Waiting

Anne Maybury

Thorndike Press • Thorndike, Maine

Library of Congress Cataloging in Publication Data:

Maybury, Anne.
  Someone waiting.

  1. Large type books. I. Title.
[PR6063.A885S6 1983]   823'.914   82-19601
ISBN 0-89621-422-2   (large print)

Large Print edition available through arrangement with Harold Ober Associates, New York.

Cover design by Armen Kojoyian.

Someone Waiting

I

Leonie heard the taxi swish away over the wet road as she let herself into the tall, narrow house in a Kensington square. Her flat was on the attic floor, looking into the trees — just a living-room, a bedroom, a kitchen and a bathroom the size of a cupboard.

When she opened her door, she could see her suitcases standing ready packed in the hall. Switching on the living-room lights, she flung off her coat and lit a cigarette, wishing desperately that something would happen even now, at the very last minute, to prevent her going away.

The flat already looked unlived-in, without flowers and the happy paraphernalia of a loved home. Against her will she was going away for a month because of a peremptory summons from an old woman she had never met — her grandmother, Venetia Sarat.

As the time drew nearer for her to leave, her dread increased. Common sense told her that there was nothing now to be afraid of. Yet there it was, the old fear, linked to the house on Richmond Hill.

I am going back to the house where Marcus was killed.

She had wandered across to the mirror over the mantel-piece. It gave her a picture of herself; a girl with an arresting face that was without real beauty. Smooth chestnut hair parted in the middle and lifted on wings at her temples; wide-spaced hazel eyes and a mouth that was deeply curved.

A newspaper had once selected six young actresses and analysed their features. Leonie was one of those chosen. When they came to her, they wrote: "A very beautiful mouth; sensitive, passionate." Passionate? About what? Her work? Her career? Certainly not about love! She turned her face away, clamping down on the old hurt that was stirring in her mind. Every girl, she told herself, had some unhappy love memory. It was part of living. . . .

At twenty-four, with dreams of being an actress, she had had to fight every inch of the way; every scrap of her success had been hardly bought. But at last she was beginning to be greeted by agents with a smile instead of a dead-pan: *"You* again?" look; beginning to have telephone calls: "Oh, Miss Sarat, there's a part we'd like to discuss with you. If you could call —"

She moved restlessly round her room.

It was charming — at least, it pleased her. Everything in it had been chosen carefully with pride, with taste, with a little fun and an eye on her fluctuating bank balance.

Once, when a friend had commented on the charm of it, admiring the choice of colour, Leonie had said:

"It's like a dish of salad, isn't it? Tomato and lettuce and cream cheese!"

That was exactly its colouring, but the result was of light and gaiety. A room to be lived-in, to laugh in, to relax in. Not that, to-night, she would find rest anywhere! For nothing could still her foreboding, her sense of the inexorableness of the living past; her feeling of utter "alone-ness" in essentials.

Between now, and when I enter this room again, what will happen? Nothing! Nothing, that is, that isn't the pattern of your life. You will have got through another few weeks of hectic rehearsals; you'll have appeared in a television play; and you will have found that time softens even the most dreadful of memories and you can bear to live again in the house on Richmond Hill. . . .

Her eyes scanned the photographs on her bureau, searching in vain for a beloved and familiar face still somewhere in the world belonging to her. She had many friends, but no close relatives. Her mother, her father, and her adored Uncle Dick were all dead.

And Marcus is dead, too, though his was never a beloved face.

There was, of course, Francie her cousin, but she had not seen her for nearly a year; there were a few aunts and uncles up in Scotland from whom she had Christmas cards and whose faces she would not know if she saw them in the street.

And then her eye fell on the letter on her desk. She walked over to it and stood for a moment looking at the scrawled page which was the reason she was returning for a month to Marcus's house.

"You will be surprised to hear from me," her grandmother had written. "Now that your grandfather is dead, I have left New Orleans and settled in England. After all, it is my country.

I want to meet my English family and so I am asking you all to stay with me for a few weeks. You first, Leonie, because you have chosen my career and so you interest me more than any of the others.

I shall expect you on Thursday, May the 3rd."

The address at the top of the letter was Heron House, Marcus's old home on Richmond Hill! The signature was large and surprisingly strong for a woman of over eighty. She signed herself with her stage name, "Venetia Sarat." It was as though, now that she was back in the country where she had been so famous as an actress, she wanted to be remembered that way and not as the wife of the rich American, Richard van Darren.

Leonie had written, welcoming her unknown grandmother, promising to come and see her but explaining that with rehearsals for a new play taking up so much of her day, she could not, for the moment at least, stay so far out. It was the only excuse she could think of for not going back.

Old Venetia promptly telephoned her.

"What rubbish is this? You can reach the theatre and the West End quite easily from here."

"But I have rehearsals every day!"

"You talk as though the house were at John o' Groats! Actresses have to be physically tough, Leonie, I know! The journey won't hurt you. I shall expect you on the third."

11

"I'm appearing in a television play that night, Grandmother." Leonie was still resisting.

"Very well. Tell me what time you will be free and I'll send a car for you."

It was no use. Leonie learned from the very start that you did not cross Venetia Sarat. . . .

And now, waiting for that car, she lived again the panic of that afternoon just over a year ago when she had entered the house on Richmond Hill and found Marcus lying dead. For a moment she felt choked so that she put her hand tightly round her throat to try and press the memory away.

Stop being scared, she told herself angrily. It's all over; it was all over a year ago . . . !

She crossed the room and opened her handbag. The only way to stop nerves was to think of something else, something pleasant. Perched on the arm of a rose-cushioned chair, she took out an envelope of her favourite cuttings about herself. She kept them always with her; pulling them out and reading them to give herself courage while she waited for some agents' interview or an audition.

The cuttings were clipped together. She flicked them over.

"Leonie Sarat has promise" . . . "The older ones among us will remember that great actress, Venetia Sarat. And now her grand-daughter, Leonie Sarat, reveals the promise of more than a little inherited talent . . . She is young, she had much to learn, but . . ."

Wonderful, encouraging words that she had only dreamed about on that day when, at eighteen, she had walked out of her cousin Marcus's house declaring that she would make her own way in life.

It was one of those times which had remained in her memory. She could recall even now her own haughty anger; the way Marcus had swivelled round in his chair and faced her, his strange light eyes mocking, his mouth hard and smiling, asking:

"And how do you propose to keep yourself?"

"I shall manage!"

"Manage" had been the operative word, she thought now with wry amusement. For a long time it had been about all she could do! "Manage" the rent; "manage" to buy herself a few clothes; "manage" to eat. And then had come her chance in repertory and the long, exacting struggle to get parts in West End plays.

She found that a snapshot had got caught up in the cuttings she was leafing through. It was of a small, laughing girl in a sun-dress and for a background there was a patio and a fountain.

Her cousin Francie Peterson. A warm feeling curled round Leonie. Francie had been on almost a year's visit to her parents in the Argentine but there had been a letter recently saying she would be home soon. She had written in her sloping scrawl:

"Mother and Father seem to be loving it out here and it really is most beautiful. But I want to get home. They don't understand, of course! They think I'm a little odd to choose to return to London to work when I could stay here and luxuriate my life away. But you know me, Leonie! I loved that youth hostel where I worked and I want to find another job like it."

There had been pages and pages to that letter, as though Fran was spending her sun-lit hours wallowing nostalgically in thought and anticipation of a grey-skied London.

Fran had had her share of grilling, too, when Marcus was killed. They had been close friends for so long but, for the months preceding Marcus's death, they had seen little of one another, both leading exacting and vastly different lives. When, therefore they met again after the tragedy, Leonie was shocked at the change in Fran. She had explained that she had been over-working and her doctor had forced her to give up the hostel job. She had been staying with an old family servant in

Sussex and would be leaving soon for a visit to her parents in the Argentine. "Just as soon," she had said shakenly, "as the police have done questioning me!"

Leonie slid the snapshot between the press cuttings.

Suddenly the doorbell rang.

She stuffed everything back into her handbag and went to answer it, wondering vaguely what Venetia Sarat's chauffeur would be like. She flung the door open.

Against the landing light she saw him. For one frozen moment she stood speechless, staring at the dark man as though this were some cruel, ironic dream out of which she was unable to drag herself.

Still in that dream, she said his name.

"Philip!"

"Hallo, Leonie!" The ordinariness of his greeting shocked her even more. "Your grandmother asked me to fetch you. She thought it might be a bit of an ordeal for you to go down to the house alone the first time."

She saw him look beyond her to the lighted room and stood aside.

She supposed she must have said: "Please come in," because he walked into her living-room. He looked, not at the room, but at her; his eyes cool, interested, appraising.

15

"It's a long time since we met, Leonie!"

She thought for a moment that he was going to reach out and take her hand. Quickly, she turned and picked up a carved wooden box.

"Cigarette? Or no," she drew her arm back. "Of course, you always smoke your own brand."

"You remember that?"

She picked up her own half-smoked cigarette.

"Marcus taught me to remember people's likes and dislikes. He used to say it was a sign of good manners."

"You sound like a little girl repeating a lesson!" his voice held amusement.

She tried to hate him as she said: "Marcus taught me many lessons, Philip. And others I learned – from experience."

It was a little too pointed, but for the life of her she couldn't help it. Seeing Philip again had shaken her out of all her self-control. But he didn't wince at her words. He merely said, quietly:

"You haven't changed –"

"Should I – after only eighteen months?"

"Perhaps. Perhaps not. I hear you're making quite a success of your life."

"Two steps forward, and one back. That's the way it is in the theatre, unless of course you're one of those rare people who become stars overnight!" She spoke lightly, and glanced at the clock. "Shouldn't we start. I mean — it's already late —"

"Of course."

He went into the hall. "Are these your suitcases?"

"Yes."

"I'll take them down to the car."

"Thank you. I'll just see that everything is locked up and then follow you down."

But for a moment after he left, she didn't move. Out of all the people in the world, it had to be Philip, the man she had loved — and tried to hate — who came to her front door that night.

She had a feeling that it wasn't just coincidence; it couldn't be *that* odd! There was a reason. After all, Philip's family had been linked professionally with the Sarats' for at least three generations.

She moved through the flat, securing windows, turning out lights.

Throughout her life in the house on Richmond Hill, she had had occasional glimpses of Philip Drew who was junior partner in the firm of lawyers which handled Marcus's affairs and had looked after old Venetia's business affairs before she had married and gone to America. Passing each other in the hall of Heron House, meeting for a moment on the steps at times when Philip had come to see Marcus, Leonie and he had smiled, greeted one another – and that was all.

So, when she had met him at a charity party given in aid of the Musicians' Fund, they knew one another's names, their jobs in life – and little else.

The party had been held in a beautiful house just outside London. The gardens, with their flowers and their lights and their fountains, were like an Arabian Night's dream. And, in that perfect setting, Leonie and Philip had really met, had talked and laughed – and fallen in love.

The whole evening was so magical that she did not question the fact that their love was mutual. It was a night for miracles.

She had cried softly. "But *is* this real? Or are we moonstruck?"

And Philip had tilted her face and made her wish on the moon.

"I wish," she had whispered to herself, "that tonight could last for ever!"

It had lasted, however, just long enough for her to know its priceless worth to her.

She tried to calm her hammering heart, to pull herself together, telling herself that remembering the past helped no one. But the relentless memory seized her in its grip.

For nearly three weeks after that first real meeting, there had been scarcely a day when they hadn't seen one another. They went to theatres, Philip amused by her acute professional interest in each actress's performance; encouraging her in her belief that one day she too would be playing in London. They drove into the country and spent long hours on the high downs, not speaking much, content with each other's company; they dined, they danced.

Then came the day when she was offered a small part in a play which was going on tour before opening in the West End.

With her new-found happiness and love flowering in her, Leonie had been reluctant to leave London, but Philip had urged her to go.

"It's the chance you've been waiting for, Leonie. Of course you're going to take it!"

And, believing that they had the whole of their lives together, Leonie had gone.

One evening during the last week of the tour, Philip rang her.

"Leonie? I've got news for you. I'm flying to New York in the morning. I have to represent a client in this big Asholme-Borlemann case. I don't know how long I'll be away, but I'll be writing."

19

She said lightly: "I'll miss you, Philip! Bring me back a bucking bronco!"

"And a cow-girl's outfit, and a lasso! But I'll be stuck in New York, sweet, fighting for my client's right to half a million dollars!"

Leonie tried to fight down the foreboding that gathered over her like a great cloud.

She heard Philip say:

"Take care of yourself, darling. And good luck with the play."

Her own voice sounded small and thin like a ghost's as she said:

"I love you, Philip! Good-bye."

The play opened in London to moderately good reviews and settled down to a fairly successful run. As soon as she had returned to town, Leonie found herself a small flat nearer the West End. She had left her forwarding address and when no letters came from Philip, she telephoned her old landlady. There was nothing there, either, from New York.

She refused to believe that the whole affair had been merely an impulse which was now crowded out of Philip's mind; that his intense desire to win his client's battle in the complicated American case had become the only thing of interest to him.

At last, in despair, she went to Heron House to ask Marcus if he had heard from Philip.

He was as delighted as ever to see her; gave her a beautifully-cooked dinner; showed her an eighteenth century bureau he had just bought, talked about his music, about the new concerto, and watched her. She knew that he sensed something was the matter and he was waiting for her to tell him.

At last she asked him if he had heard from Philip. Casually, as if it didn't matter very much, she said that she had met him a few times in London and that she would like his address in New York if Marcus by any chance knew it. "Just," she went on, "to send him a 'Good Luck' message. The case he's on sounds complicated —"

Leonie could act before an audience but she couldn't get away with pretence with Marcus! He was too wise in the ways of the world. He fixed those light-gold eyes of his on her and said:

"So you've been out with Philip Drew? He's a very efficient young lawyer, Leonie. But why this extreme interest?"

He didn't need an answer; his expression told her she hadn't fooled him by her casualness.

"For heaven's sake, don't let yourself fall in love with him!" he said sharply. "I believe he has quite a way with women! And you're too young to be playing with fire."

21

But she had gone on, refusing to believe that a man could lie so convincingly about love, holding Philip's words close in her heart. And then, at last, when no letter came, she had to face the fact that Marcus, as usual, had been damnably right and she would never hear of Philip again. . . .

She slammed the kitchen door.

How *could he? How dare* he come to fetch her to-night! Or had he thought those enchanted evenings had meant no more to her than they had to him? Had he just seen her as a sophisticated young actress playing a role in a setting that cried out for all the romance you could give it? Had he thought her avid for "all experience"? A lover of life "Ready to be anything in the ecstasy of being ever?"

She switched off the hall lights, closed her flat door and went down the stairs of the silent house.

In the car, she sat by Philip's side, her hands clasped; a gold bracelet gleaming at her wrist and the collar of her big sapphire coat turned up round her throat.

She tried not to feel shaken by his nearness.

Philip was saying:

". . . and so you'd better know how I came to be fetching you. You see, when your grand-mother returned to England a few months ago,

22

she contacted us, as we are the family lawyers. You know, of course, how she came by the house, don't you?"

Philip continued: as though he hadn't seen her nod.

"Marcus's wife, Diana, inherited everything, in spite of having divorced him. He had never made a new will so even that house became hers. She didn't want it — she's happily married now with three children, so she sold it back to your grandmother."

"It was originally grandmother's home."

"Yes. And some weeks after she arrived, she sent for me to handle her complicated American-English affairs," he laughed, steered the car skilfully round a crawling bus, and went on. "She says she favours young lawyers; old ones, she insists, are too keen to get home and put their feet up!"

"What is she like?"

"You'll see for yourself very soon now!"

"But to pull up roots — after forty years in America! And at eighty —"

"It makes one wonder at what age people grow old, doesn't it?"

They were rapidly approaching Richmond Hill and two emotions tore at her — the realisation that she still loved Philip and the curious, premonitory panic that something evil was awaiting her at Heron House.

"Stop being scared, Leonie!"

She sat up, startled. "I —"

"Don't pretend you're not! I can feel it."

"It doesn't make sense, does it?" she said hopelessly.

"It makes sense because I hear you haven't set foot in Heron House since the tragedy, have you?"

"Even so —"

"It's like falling off a horse. You have to get on again immediately, otherwise you lose your nerve. If you had gone back —"

"I couldn't!"

"No, I suppose not! You loved him too much, didn't you, Leonie?"

"*Loved* him?" She heard her own voice, full of shaken surprise. And then she checked the wild denial. Of course they would all of them expect her to love Marcus out of gratitude — as you loved parents and brothers and sisters. She supposed Philip couldn't understand that Marcus was not a person anyone could love. . . .

"And now," he continued matter-of-factly, "you're going back again — and that's all there is to it. You're going to break the nightmare, Leonie. If your grandmother can live there, so can you."

24

"It's different for her; she can't have known Marcus well, except during the period when he went to the States. I think if the whole mystery had been cleared up and we had known who — who killed him, I wouldn't feel like this about it. It's the not knowing —"

"You never will, now!"

"I wonder. Sometimes, something happens which throws a light on an old mystery. I have a feeling that, in that house, I'll find something — some clue —"

"Don't!" he said sharply, "don't think like that! It means that you'll never be able to put the affair into the past, and that won't help your career, or Marcus, now!"

"It's like an urge I can't control," she cried. "I suppose it's because I was involved."

"If everyone down the pages of history let themselves be haunted by the mysteries and the violence around them, they would probably have created a race of ghosts!"

She saw that he either could not, or would not, understand. Quietly, she changed the subject.

"Who's at Heron House?"

"Julian, your grandmother's adopted son, and his wife. And Fran —"

"Fran!" Warmth flowed over her. "So she's back. The little beast, and she never let me know!"

Philip said ruefully, "She arrived a few days ago and she wanted to surprise you, and now I've spoilt it."

"Oh Philip you haven't! You couldn't! It's good to know I'll have someone to hold hands with! How is she?"

"Very tanned, and her brown hair's bleached by the sun. She seems somehow – excited."

"That's because she's back. She was getting restless out in the Argentine. Fran's always had a mission in life – looking after the young –" Leonie laughed, "as though she isn't young herself!"

Philip was slowing down, peering along the roadside.

"I wonder if there's a telephone kiosk round these parts? I want to ring Claire."

Because she was still thinking of Fran, the name didn't register.

"Claire?"

"You remember her. She was Claire Fermaine; her father was a partner in the firm before he died and her grandfather used to look after your grandmother's affairs when she was on the London stage. Claire married Johnnie Lavall –" He broke off, took his cigarette case out of his pocket and, when she refused one, lit his own expertly with his left hand, the other guiding the car.

Leonie thought: He smokes too much!

"I knew Claire slightly some years ago," she said.

Philip was driving slowly, peering ahead of him, leaning forward a little. She had a wild urge to break all conventions, to pocket pride, to know the truth; to cry: "Remember me? I was the girl you said you loved! What happened, Philip? What went wrong?"

"Claire," he was saying, "had a bad accident. Did you know?"

"No. How could I? I never see anyone now who knows her. I can't afford lawyers myself, anyway."

"You will. One day you'll be rich. I've seen you on television, and I saw you in that play, *Carving in Ivory.*"

"Such a small part —"

"But one that drew special mention from the critics!"

"What happened — about Claire?" she dragged the conversation away from herself.

"She was involved in a car smash. It affected her left leg and she is very lame."

"I'm sorry. I'd have gone to see her if I'd known! Oh Philip, how terrible for her — I seem to remember she loves beauty so much!"

"It was horrible but the worst is over now. Her marriage was disastrous, as you probably

27

know. When Johnnie left her, she went to work for Edward de Crispin, the interior decorator."

"She was always very clever artistically. I believe she studied at the Slade. You say the worst is over?"

"She is still having treatment twice a week and, after preparatory work is done, there is to be an operation on her leg. They say it will be perfectly successful. But in the meantime, it is all very difficult for her — and extremely painful."

"And you want to — to telephone her?"

(*Why? Why*)

"Your grandmother asked me to bring her to Heron House; she wanted to see what old Brand Fermaine's granddaughter looked like. When she learned about the accident and heard that Claire had to climb three flights of stairs to her flat, very much against her doctor's wishes, she suggested that Claire should come and live at Heron House until the operation in a couple of months' time."

"And Claire accepted?"

"She jumped at the idea. She is supposed to be arriving to-night, but she and de Crispin are working on a house in Sussex and she said she might be very late. She has her own little car but I thought perhaps I could help her with her suitcases if she is home. I can't fetch her

28

because she will be coming in her own car — she'll need it at Heron House — but I rang her just before I called for you and she wasn't in then. There's a kiosk. Do you mind if I just put a call through again?"

"Of course not."

He drew into the side of the road and switched off the engine. His hand was on the handle of the door as he said, looking straight ahead of him.

"By the way, in four month's time, the three-year period for desertion will be ended and Claire will be free of Johnnie. She and I are planning to get married."

Leonie didn't move; didn't even turn her head as Philip crossed to the telephone kiosk. She sat thinking shakenly, that if this had been a stage play, the curtain would have come down on that announcement. As it was, this was real life and there was no curtain; just the street lights shining on the dark road and the heedless traffic tearing by. . . .

Philip is going to marry Claire Fermaine. Or no, that wasn't her name now. Claire Lavall, Johnnie's deserted wife. . . .

A car swished past, its tires screaming, hissing at her.

Philip is going to marry Claire. . . .

Had he deliberately chosen this moment to

tell her, when he could leave her to digest the fact without him? If so, why?

Because he knew she *had* to know before they reached the house on Richmond Hill, and he hadn't the moral courage to be sitting near her while he told her? But why again? Because he still felt the guilt of those evenings so long ago? If it were that, then she must show him his news hadn't touched her — that the past was quite dead for her. . . . She was an actress, after all, she should know how to play the sophisticated role of tossing off a romantic affair with a quip. . . .

Only he had saved her that by leaving her at the moment of telling. . . .

Then came the full realisation of what it meant to her. Claire would be staying at Heron House and Philip would come and see her there!

I shall have the present as well as the past to cope with! Philip and Claire . . . and the ghost of Marcus!

Why wasn't this the moment when one could be ill? Faint. Be rushed off to hospital? Why couldn't there be a call from her agent to-morrow telling her that there was a part for her on Broadway, New York, and that she was released from her part in the play at the Shelton Theatre? Why couldn't something happen to stop her going to Heron House?

But miracles didn't happen. You were knocked flat and you just had to pick yourself up, brush yourself down and say with a smile "I'm all right! I'm fine!"

She was aware that Philip had returned and was opening the car door.

"Claire isn't home yet. So we'll go on."

Richmond Hill was almost in sight. The car accelerated and slid smoothly up the beautiful, familiar road.

Leonie focused hard on it, trying to shut out her memory of Claire as she had last seen her, some years ago. But she would not *be* shut out! Small and pale, with her subtly appealing face, her mixture of artistic talent and practical application, she was to Leonie, an innocent — and secretly so bitter — usurper. The picture that was in her mind, though was not quite accurate. She must try to visualise her no longer with that smooth, gliding step but walking with difficulty, in pain: visualise her too, as the girl Philip loved. . . .

Ahead of her, Leonie could see now the curve of the high surrounding wall of Heron House that had once been her cousin Marcus's small and elegant home, looking out over its cloistered garden to the river. A lamp at the kerbside shone on to the stone bird

31

that gave the house its name.

Philip turned the car into the semi-circular drive.

"The house looks festive enough!" he observed. "All lit up!"

"Like a stage-set, ready for the drama to begin!"

"Hey, don't get imaginative!" He was laughing.

The car stopped and Leonie got out. The ancient oaks stood black against the stars. She smelt the scent of a garden in the night, lilac blossom and the lambent, rainwashed smell of grass.

Philip put out a hand and she felt him touch her arm.

"Don't stop for a moment to get nerves! Hurry! Hurry! I'll bring in your cases."

She drew away from him. This, she told herself, was the worst moment. Afterwards, when the ice was broken, everything would be all right. At least she must think that, else she would turn and run from that short flight of steps up which, a year ago, she had watched the police come to question her, to look at a dead man and find the weapon, the little, inscrutable stone cat. . . .

II

At the top of the steps, a huge smiling negress was waiting for her.

"M's Venetia am in de drawin' room, Ma'am —"

Leonie said, "Thank you," gave her smile for smile and went into the wide hall.

The valuable silken, hanging carpets glowed from the walls. Slowly Leonie's eyes moved around them, remembering their Eastern names — Shiraz and Isfahan and Samarkand.

Marcus had treasured his carpets and had arranged them so that the hall lights would show up their rich, jewel colours.

Apart from them, nothing was the same. The house was more brilliantly lit, had more colour but less subtle perfection.

The furniture was ornate; a woman's choice of seventeenth century extravaganza; ormolu and inlay, sconces on the wall held by gilded cupids, golden fauns carved on cabriole legs of tables, garlanded mirrors. In this age of simplicity, it was like walking into a room at a museum.

Leonie stood for a moment remembering Marcus's exquisite taste.

"Leonie?"

She started violently and lifted her head.

"Is that you, Leonie?" called a voice from above. "We are all up here. Boadicea will see to your luggage. Come along. Is Philip with you?"

"Present!" Philip raised his voice and set the suitcases down in the hall.

Leonie walked up the fine, familiar staircase with the head of a blackamoor for a newel post. Her footsteps were silent on the thick crimson carpet. That was new, too! Marcus hated red!

Entering the large, high-ceilinged room on the first floor, Leonie's gaze went straight to the woman by the mantelpiece.

Most octogenarians would sit to welcome young relatives. Venetia Sarat stood. She gave a sensation of largeness though she was a small woman. She held herself with pride, back erect. Her hair was fine and snow-white, piled on top of her head; her eyes had an almost feline light-gold watchfulness. They're Marcus's eyes, Leonie thought, and forgot for a moment that he was dead.

Venetia watched her walk across the room as though this were an audition and she the selector. She was a very still person; the sheen of her dark green velvet dress did not quiver, so that her breathing must be very light.

"So you are Leonie?"

As the lined face lifted a little and dry lips touched Leonie's cheek in a greeting, she wondered what to call her. "Grannie" was too warmly familiar; "Gran" too casual; "Grandmother" a mouthful, but for the present the only solution.

"I'm sorry I'm late, but I *did* suggest coming tomorrow."

"Late? At half-past ten?" Old Venetia seemed to take it as a personal affront. "If anyone wishes to go to bed, they may. I shall stay up."

The four people gathered there did not move. Leonie felt their eyes on her. Her gaze caught and held one pair of smiling brown eyes. Fran Peterson! Thank heaven for that one fond and friendly face!

The two girls moved towards one another in a swift greeting.

"Leonie!"

"You brat!" Leonie hugged her. "Not telling me you were home!"

"I wanted it to be a surprise. I knew we'd both be coming here."

"I forgive you. That tan of yours looks almost too good to be true!" Leonie wanted to go on talking to Fran, but she turned politely towards her grandmother.

"Do you know your relatives on your father's side?" Venetia asked.

Leonie shook her head.

"We're a scattered family, but they're all coming to stay soon. Your cousin Dorcas and her husband, your Aunt Marian and her daughter, your cousin Lena —"

"I know their hand-writing from their Christmas cards," Leonie laughed, "but I've never met them."

"It's just as well," Venetia retorted. "They're probably dull — my husband's English relatives were all unspeakably dreary!" she turned. "In the meantime, you haven't met Julian."

He was the young man whom Leonie remembered hearing Venetia had adopted. He came forward, thin, fair, handsome with a slightly weak face and a charming smile.

"We've been hearing about you from Venetia," he said and took her hand. "You'd be surprised how she's kept tabs on you over all those thousands of miles! You're following in her footsteps, aren't you, and making a name for yourself."

"Only a small one. But the critics have been kind."

"Kind?" snapped Venetia. "The critics are

never kind! They're not paid to be. They recognise talent, that's all." Her eyes flicked over her granddaughter. Then, turning her head, she said: "And this is Hilda, Julian's wife."

She had an actress's gift for inferring what even she did not dare say; but it was all too clear. "This," she might have said, "is a minion; someone not to be reckoned with! Julian's Folly!"

Leonie smiled at Hilda. She was small, with pretty fair hair and a sensitive mouth. She moved restlessly; her handshake was jerky and her eyes had the pink-rimmed look of someone who had been crying.

Venetia produced champagne. While Boadicea, panting and beaming, brought in glasses on a silver tray, Venetia said:

"I've put you in the corner room with the river view, Leonie."

"Thank you." (And thank heaven, she thought, that she was not being given her old room, the one with the memories!)

Philip popped the champagne cork. Fran moved to Leonie's side. She looked, as Philip had said, tanned and plump and well and the Argentine sun had produced attractive streaks of silvery beige in her light brown hair.

She wore a beautiful dress of dark blue silk

and her necklace was a real topaz strung between gold links. But then Fran's parents were rich.

"I want to hear all your news," Leonie whispered.

"Me, too!" Fran said, tone-deaf to grammar.

Philip was pouring champagne into beautiful cut glass; Julian was handing the drinks around. He stood in front of Leonie and looked at her and smiled. She took the glass, said "Thank you" and smiled back.

"I need something like this," Fran said in a low voice to Leonie. "I've only been in this house a few hours, but it's giving me the jitters!"

"Claire will be late," Venetia told them, "so we won't wait for her. I gather these people she works for keep her all hours."

"And allow her hours off when others are working," Philip said. "De Crispin is a very fair employer and anyway, Claire loves her work."

"Philip and Claire are to be married when she is able to divorce that runaway husband of hers," Venetia said.

"Yes, I know." Leonie turned deliberately and glanced round the room and saw that the colour red predominated and that there was a great deal of french ormolu about. Venetia was still faithful, then, to the plush and gilt of her day! She wondered vaguely what had happened to Marcus's elegant pieces. Diana had probably sold them — Marcus had once said that Diana had hated the house because everything was too perfect in it.

"Julian is interested in the stage, too," Venetia was saying. "Both his parents were straight actors."

"But there was nothing straight about me!" he interposed lightly. "I twisted every character I tried to play, so I was told. Quite unconsciously, through sheer nerves, really, I 'guyed' everything. but even so, I was never funny! Venetia was furious. I suspect she only adopted me because she hoped she could bask in my glory!"

A light, friendly battle ensued between them. Leonie stopped listening.

So this, she thought, is the boy whom Venetia took into her house at the age of fourteen! And there, sitting near him, was his wife.

Hilda was leaning forward, listening to their light wrangling, putting in little stabs of words herself and being ignored. Hilda's eyes dropped and lifted, glanced about her and always came back to Venetia.

She's afraid of her, Leonie thought. She must

have been in her early thirties and her round pale face that should have been chubby and happy had strained, down-drooping lines.

Sitting there, talking, drinking champagne to celebrate the meeting, Leonie felt the room over-charged with a kind of secretiveness. She tried to puzzle out from whom it came and gradually it dawned on her that it emanated from their mutual refusal to mention Marcus's name. It was as though, by agreement before she came, they eliminated him, thus making his presence and the mystery of his death more sharply felt. Even Fran seemed implicated, guarded against her and anything she might say, the pretty, tanned face alert, the slender body unrelaxed.

But this was nonsense! This had been Marcus's house; his brilliant life had been led here! He belonged, he was of their blood and he had suffered a violent death. . . .

The conversation flowed, with Venetia leading it. Leonie knew that they were all aware of her silence, of the way she watched them. She felt they were frightened of her, of what she might say, and this feeling roused a rebellion in her. *None of you would be here, in this beautiful house, if Marcus hadn't been killed!* Love him? Oh, no, nobody could quite have done that! Pay respect to him? How Marcus would have laughed at that phrase! Remember him? That was it!

Suddenly, unbidden and startlingly the urge became irresistible. She heard herself say in a high, clear voice that had undertones of anger:

"I suppose it's different for all of you, but to me the house is full of Marcus. He's *here,* with us! Don't you feel it? *Can't* you?" The words froze as she felt their resentment mobilised against her.

There was a long silence. Hilda put her hand to her mouth; Julian tense; Fran's face seemed to tighten; Philip looked into his champagne glass.

Someone speak soon, Leonie thought. *Someone say something!*

"You should know your Shakespeare," Venetia said at last. " 'What's done is done!' The dreadful past has no echo after all this time and any feelings you have that seem to — er — haunt you are all in your imagination." She looked around the room and asked a little testily: "Where is my footstool? All these chairs are too large for me."

It was, Leonie knew, a deliberate diversion. But so strong was the strange urge inside her that it was almost as though the will of Marcus himself drove her to force them to remember him in this, his home.

The little play with the footstool was over. Leonie heard her own voice, impelled by that hidden force.

"I'm sorry, Grandmother, but you see if whoever killed Marcus had been discovered and brought to justice, then I could say: 'What's done is done!' But no one was ever found. It's like a story only half told. And if, somehow, it could be finished —"

"Are you inferring," there was a glint of impatience in Venetia's old eyes, "that we should become amateur detectives and try to avenge Marcus's death by setting ourselves to find his killer?"

"No, of course not!" (And yet, perhaps that was what something inside her was urging!) "Did you know very much about it all?" she asked. "Did the story reach New Orleans?"

"My lawyers wrote to me at the time. As Marcus's lawyers, too, they had to. And I ordered all the English newspapers to learn as much as I could. I wrote to you, Leonie, and told you how very shocked I was —"

"Yes, you did."

"And now," Julian put in quickly, "it's all over and done with. The case is closed."

"You don't know English police methods," she said quickly, "if you think they ever close the files on an undiscovered murder. And somewhere in this house there *could* be a clue. Even now, after all this time, perhaps we shall find out who killed —"

"If the police couldn't, then you can be certain *you* won't be able to." Julian rushed in as though trying to stop her saying the name again.

Marcus's name must not be mentioned! They watched her as though she were a child wanting to play a dangerous game.

Leonie tried to understand. Of course, *they've* got to live here — they don't feel as I do, so they just want to blot the whole thing out.

Old Venetia was saying:

"When you reach my age, you'll realise that wherever you walk, you walk with ghosts. You learn to live with them," her eyes became wise, her tone changed. "I suppose your obsession with that tragic affair is natural, since you and Marcus — well —" she paused, smiled and added, "You see, my dear, your secret travelled across oceans!"

"My — *secret?*" Leonie felt her whole being brace itself for some shock. "I don't know what you're talking about."

"That you and Marcus were going to be married, of course! You were, weren't you?"

"*No!*"

But Venetia seemed not to hear her violent denial.

"It would probably have been an excellent thing. Marcus was much too domineering to live happily with a woman of his own age. But he had brought you up, trained you to think and act and live *his* way. So—"

"Please don't go on!" Leonie could dominate too. Her voice filled the room, but there was nothing theatrical about it. "It's all utterly wrong. It's almost — funny! Only nothing seems to be funny any more." Her voice lost its ringing power and she was despairingly aware of Philip sitting across the room.

"But my dear," Venetia's voice held a puzzled note, "we always thought —"

"I don't know how such a rumour started, but there was *never* any question of my marrying Marcus. I was grateful for all he did for me, but that was all." Her gaze, turning from her grandmother's bright, listening face, met Philip's eyes. She saw with a shock that he didn't believe her.

"Fran —" she cried, seeking her cousin's eyes. "You know there was nothing, absolutely nothing, between Marcus and me. There never was —"

"No," Fran said a little vaguely. "I didn't *think* there was. But he was always so secretive, he enjoyed intriguing people."

"You never thought for one moment that Marcus and I – that there was any understanding of marriage?" Leonie insisted.

Fran said unhappily. *"You* never said anything, Leonie, but –"

"But what?" Leonie dragged out of her.

"Well," her pretty, distressed eyes lifted to Leonie's face and met the almost violent questioning look. "Marcus did say – that – that if he married again, you were the only woman he'd choose as his second wife."

Leonie sat where she was, making no movement, momentarily blind to their listening faces. Then she said very quietly:

"You all seem to know far more about his thoughts and his feelings than I ever did!"

"I don't know why you're making such a fuss about it," Venetia almost snapped. "All right, so you weren't going to marry Marcus! But why behave as though it were a most outrageous suggestion? Marcus was an attractive man, and brilliant and rich –"

She watched her granddaughter. Leonie didn't speak, she didn't look up from her study of the bright carpet which replaced Marcus's beautiful Eastern rugs. But she was desperately aware of Philip, aware of the moment when he stirred, as though he'd had enough of this conversation.

45

"I've got a hard day to-morrow. I must be getting along. Oh, and by the way, Leonie, I found a scarf in the car. I don't know if it's yours. Perhaps you'll come down with me and see."

She had left no scarf in his car and he must know it!

"My two are packed, so the one you found must be Claire's."

Venetia made a small movement with her hand.

"Well, you'd better go down and make sure. And find out if Boadicea has taken your luggage to your room. Oh, and tell her that I'm on my way to bed and will she bring up my Thermos of milk?"

"Of course, Grandmother."

Leonie walked past Philip out of the door, went down the wide staircase and heard him say:

"I took your cases to your room. Boadicea told me where you were sleeping."

"Thank you."

When they reached the hall, Leonie murmured: "Good night, Philip," and walked along the passage to the kitchen.

Boadicea was sitting, voluminous skirt round her knees, reading a lurid-looking paper-back novel. She raised her black face as she heard the tap of Leonie's heels, slapped down her book and rose with a beaming smile.

"You wantin' someptin', M's Sarat?"

Leonie gave her Venetia's message and then went back down the hall.

Coming from the darkened passage, it was like a stage-set, brilliant, rococo and gilded as a Louis d'Or *salon*.

And standing quietly in the centre of all that theatricality, was Philip.

He looked up as she came and moved to her side.

"I thought you'd gone," she said flatly.

"I've been waiting for you. I want to talk to you."

"I'm sorry, Philip, but I'm rather tired."

He took her arm.

"Not too tired to spare me five minutes."

"Very well. What do you want to say?"

"Come outside."

She resisted the slight pull on her arm:

"We can talk here. It'll be cold in the garden."

"If it is, I'll get the rug from the car and wrap it round you."

She couldn't resist any longer the quiet authority of his manner. Together they walked away from the lights and into the silence and the darkness of the garden.

The night air was soft; a half-moon shone on the tall lupins and the beds of escallonia, washing them of colour. The air was sweet with wallflowers.

Philip paused by the sunken garden with the small fountain. He put one foot on the stone plinth, staring at the little dancing spurts of water.

"Why didn't you want your grandmother to know about your proposed marriage to Marcus?"

"Because there was never any question of it. I told the truth."

He swung round, his head bent, trying to see her face as she stood with her back to the moonlight.

"Leonie —"

"I'm sorry if you don't believe me." She had her arms wrapped tightly round her body, holding herself in, holding herself steady. . . .

"But Marcus himself told me!"

For one moment she couldn't speak; it was as though he had struck a blow at her, his statement telling her that she lied. *Marcus told me!*"

"You — you must have misunderstood something he said —" Her voice was frigid with controlled nerves.

"This was something I could never

misunderstand, Leonie! Marcus told me in simple words a child could comprehend that one day soon you were going to marry him."

"But it wasn't true! I told Grandmother, I'm telling *you* – I would never have married Marcus, not in a million years!"

Philip seized her arms and his grip hurt.

"What happened?"

"Philip, what's the use of questions, now? It's all over!"

"I thought it was, too, but it seems I was wrong. It seems we both have to do some explaining."

"I have nothing to explain, " she said in a small, weary voice, "and I'm tired. I've had a long day. Let me go, please –" she was trembling and she knew he could feel it.

"We're going to talk this out. You're tired. I'm sorry, but I'm going to be hard. I've got to know, Leonie. I've got to have the truth.

"I've told you the truth –"

"All right! And now you're going to hear my story. It'll hurt – *me*, I mean. But it's got to be said. Leonie, when I reached New York I found I hadn't got that piece of paper with your address on. I had been in such a hurry the night before. I'd sat up until nearly four in the morning studying the case I was to work on and so I had to get my father's old batman to pack for me. He valeted my things and must have found the piece of paper with your address on and either thrown it away or let it slip out unnoticed. So, when I wrote you from New York I had to send the letters here, care of Marcus. I wrote three times. Then I telephoned Marcus from the States to ask him where you were living. He told me about your unofficial engagement to him."

"But he *can't* have done! There wasn't —"

"Marcus told me," he interrupted roughly, "that you were going to marry him. I didn't believe him. Do you know what he said? 'Leonie's an actress first and foremost. She's very inclined to act a life-scene, romantic or dramatic, as though she's on the stage. But I must say this for her, she's practical! She knows the value of a background, the sort *I* can give her. And when she's had her little fling, she's going to settle down and marry me.' He also said: "You see, *I* understand her. You don't."

"I wasn't going to marry Marcus. Philip you must have known —"

"After that transatlantic talk, I even wrote to you again. I sent the letter care of the office asking them to get it to you somehow. They must have sent that letter, too, to Heron House. I never asked them when I returned —

what was the use? I wanted to forget you!"

"Your office couldn't have found me — unless you'd told them what play I was touring in."

"When I came back to England I was determined not to contact you. The fact that you hadn't replied to any of my letters was proof enough —"

"Philip listen! Oh, *listen!*" her voice was desperate. "I tell you — *I never received any letters from you!*"

"If you didn't — then what happened to them?"

She knew their fate.

"Marcus — must have read them — and destroyed them!"

Philip didn't move. His body was like a wall of steel taking the blow. Only, very, very softly, she thought she heard him cry. "God in heaven!"

The blow was as violent for her too. The silence beat about them while they tried to visualise that act which had broken their love. They stared at each other in the moonlight, dumb and dismayed.

"He meant to marry you!" Philip said at last.

"I don't believe he ever did until he realised that — that someone else wanted me!"

"But a man doesn't say a girl is going

to marry him unless —"

"Unless what?"

"She gives him some encouragement, some hope."

"Marcus never needed anything outside to give him hope!" she said bitterly, her voice shaking as though she were very cold. "He had all the faith in himself."

"And he wanted you."

"Not because he loved me," she managed to drag her eyes to his face, to see the stark pain lit by the cold moonlight. "Marcus was Venetia's nephew. He could act, too. I've known him have a saint's gentleness when he thought it was expedient."

"What have I done?" The four raw words were torn from him.

"Those few weeks weren't long enough for you to know me sufficiently, Philip! So you believed Marcus — the wiser, older man. It's as simple as that!"

"And then Claire came into my life. She had a raw deal — first Johnnie, and then the accident. We were both lonely, both let down — and love can grow out of pity. Mine did."

"Philip, don't let's talk about it. It can't help now. Nothing can — it's too late."

"There's one thing to be said," as he bent his head, the moonlight caught his eyes so that they were like silver. "I have never ceased to love you."

"And I –" But her voice caught in her throat. She turned quickly, and something seemed to move in the blackness of the shadowy bushes behind them. Perhaps she thought, it was a trick of vision made by the tears swimming in her eyes.

She heard Philip ask, "What are we going to do?"

She shook her head. "Nothing. This isn't something unique – something that has just happened to us! It's happened before, thousands of times. Two people love and are parted for some reason and they – they just have to go on. My grandmother said that back at the house. Don't you remember? She said: 'What's done is done.' We've just got to go on."

"Go on – without you? Now that I know the past was not your lie but Marcus's? Oh, Leonie –"

She stepped back quickly. "Don't be kind to me! Don't ever let's be – together. If we have to meet, let it be with other people!"

This time there was an unmistakable sound behind them and they both turned simultaneously.

A girl stood on the path between the flowering lilac bushes. Her dark dress melted into the matching blue-black background so that only her face and her hands seemed to be there. She looked as unreal as an unfinished painting.

"Hallo, Philip."

"Claire. I understood you wouldn't be coming until to-morrow." His voice was carefully controlled.

"Mrs. van Darren said that if I could possibly manage it I was to come to-night. I arrived very late and I saw her and she told me that you couldn't wait. You'd gone, she said." Claire had an almost little-girl way of speaking, slow and downright.

"I wanted a word with Leonie —"

"Oh hallo," Claire turned, acknowledging her at last.

Leonie took a grip on herself. "Phil did his good deed for the day and brought me here." Her voice was almost casual. "It was Grandmother's idea that I might be having nerves about coming."

"Yes?"

Had Claire just arrived, or had she been watching them for some time? She could not, surely, have heard what they were saying! Leonie watched her come forward, dragging her left leg and lifting her face to Philip's to be kissed.

"I didn't dream I'd be so late, but just when Mr. de Crispin and I were going, Julia Mandeley came in and she insisted on us staying and talking a few things over with her. We all had dinner at some inn nearby and then went back to the house. You've no idea the fuss there is about whether the ruby-red we've got is the right shade for that Italian Renaissance dining-room she wants! Then, when I got here, I saw your car in the drive so I knew that though Mrs. van Darren thought you'd gone, you hadn't. I thought you were waiting for me in the garden." Her flat little voice went on and on; her face was as white as paper.

"You look tired, Claire —"

"Thats a most unflattering remark, Philip!" her tone was soft, but anger quivered in it. "And anyway, I'm not in the least bit tired," her eyes moved from one to the other. "Come to that, *you* both look pale — as though you'd seen a ghost in this garden! But perhaps there are ghosts — or just one —" she gave a little shiver. "I'm so glad you were here, Philip, to console Leonie! It must be quite an ordeal for her, coming back!" Claire put out a hand to the lilac bush by her side and dragged her fingers along the snowy cone of blossoms. She must have torn at it for the tiny blooms fell off, scattering about her.

55

"Hey!" Philip said quickly. "Don't mutilate the garden like that or you'll have Venetia after you!"

"I've been stuffed up in a house that smells of paint," she wiped her hand down her dark dress. "I want some fresh air, Philip darling. Let's just walk down to the terrace, shall we?"

"Of course."

Leonie forced herself to utter polite "good nights." "And thanks, Philip, for pulling me up in time!"

As she turned away, she heard Claire ask:

"What did Leonie mean about you pulling her up in time?"

"I got all nervy and imaginative about the house," she called back before Philip could answer. "That's all!"

She walked quickly away without looking back. But she was trembling with the shock of knowing that Philip still loved her — and of trying to understand how he could love Claire, too. But she knew! There were degrees of loving and deepest of all was his feeling for *her*. She wished it wasn't like that. She wished his love for her had been weak and had died so that, perhaps, hers could die, too.

As it was . . . A sudden anger against Marcus flared up in her. Wanting her for himself, not to love but as a product of his upbringing, another addition to his beautiful home, to show off to his guests. . . . "You should have seen her when she came here! A skinny little girl of eight with rats' tails. *Now* look at her!"

Leonie paused for a moment on the path before the house and looked up at it. Old and beautifully proportioned, it had been built for a more solid generation. Its grey walls were almost white in the moonlight, the waxen flowers of the camellia clinging to the space between the music-room windows glowed like opaque stars.

This had been her home and here Marcus had played the music he composed. But in that moment it was not the memory of Marcus which was pictured in her mind, but the single tearing movement of Claire's broad white hand on the lilac bush. . . .

III

Inside the house, the lights still burned. Boadicea's black, beaming face appeared from the passage to the kitchen.

"You wantin' somet'in,' Mis' Sarat, before you goes to bed?"

"No thank you."

"I watched you in dat play on the telly tonight. My, but you was lovely!"

"It was an exciting play, wasn't it, Boadicea?" Leonie said kindly.

Beaming with pride at knowing someone who acted, Boadicea watched Leonie go upstairs.

Alone at last in her room, she lit a cigarette and wandered about, letting old personal memories crowd out all that was immediate.

Leonie had been only eight years old when an epidemic abroad had killed both her parents and she had come to Heron House from the boarding-school in Wiltshire.

Marcus was to be her guardian and from then on, she had spent all her holidays with him. But he had remained a stranger. He had given her neither companionship nor affection. Florrie, his housekeeper, did her best to make up to the little girl for the sudden lack of love in her life, for the tearing away of her childish sense of security when her gay, adoring parents had so suddenly died.

Not that Marcus took no interest in her. He went to a great deal of trouble to teach her to appreciate beautiful things, to take a pride in her appearance, to meet people without shyness. Only he made no effort to give her the warmth of loving, the moving wonder of compassion.

After Leonie left Heron House and set out to make her own life, she did not break entirely with Marcus. She still visited him, and the week-end before he had died she had spent at Heron House. He had been in a curious, elated mood because for some time he had been working on a theme for a piano concerto and now at last he had it. So far, he had told her, it was just a few bars in his head to be played and dreamed over at his piano but not yet committed to paper.

She seldom went down to the house on Richmond Hill two week-ends running, but the following Saturday, with nothing to do, she went for a few hours.

And there, in his music-room, she had found Marcus dead.

The doctor had put the time of death as between five o'clock and six. And the church clock had struck the quarter after six as Leonie had walked down the drive on that dark, wet evening.

Over and over again the police had asked her the same questions, "Try to remember the smallest, the most seemingly unimportant thing, Miss Sarat." "Go over every step of the way you took from the gate to the house." "Remember, Miss Sarat, just try to remember!"

Had she seen any car leaving the house? No. There were a great many passing up and down the Hill. Oh, and there had been one moving slowly along the lower road at the far end of the garden, gathering speed, it seemed. "Ah! Why did you notice it?" ... "Because not many cars use that road — it leads nowhere much." She had gone on to say that it couldn't have stopped at the house and been moving away when she saw it because only the staff knew about that back gate in the wall that led out to the lower road.

Nevertheless, the police investigated, testing with their cars and with the police doctor's high-slung one, and found that it was impossible to see, from the place where Leonie had been walking, even the top of a car passing along the lower road. The garden wall, they said, was too high. She must have seen the shadow of a tree-branch moving and the car sound must have been one from the other road, from Richmond Hill.

All they had to go on so far as Marcus's death was concerned, was the statuette of a tall-eared, ancient Egyptian cat, lying on the rug, with which Marcus had been struck. There were no fingerprints on it — not even Florrie's, who must often have dusted it. Someone had wiped it and put it back on the floor where it had fallen after striking him.

Nothing else — nothing in the whole beautiful house. . . .

"Murdered," was the verdict, "by person or persons unknown."

Everyone had thought that Leonie would inherit at least some of Marcus's wealth. But the only will he had ever made was the one soon after his marriage to Diana. By accident, or design, he had never changed it. . . .

Leonie turned from the window and switched on the room lights and began to unpack. She had barely started when there was a light tap on her door.

"It's me, Fran."

The door opened. She wore a dark tailored housecoat and red slippers and she padded to the bed and sat on it, lightly as a feather.

"I had to come in and just say how glad I am you decided to come. Oh, Leonie, I'd have hated it here without you!"

"Being among strangers – yes –"

"Not exactly that. I'm used to lots of strangers in my work. But because of the memories of – of Marcus!"

"You always rather liked him, didn't you?"

Leonie was sitting on the dressing-table stool, her hands playing with her hairbrush. Fran watched her, and said:

"I admired Marcus – in ways. He could tear your heart out when he played to you."

"That was the best part of him, his music. I think that's where all his love went and he had none left for people. But I think he liked people to love him, it stimulated him, and amused him."

"You and Philip and I are the only ones here who knew him. I suppose Grandmother must have met him when he went over to the States to play, but we were the ones closest to him." Fran splayed her square, suntanned hands. "Jim is still here."

"Jim?" Leonie thought for a moment. "Oh, you mean Jim Farraday, the gardener? Is he? I suppose Diana kept him on because she felt that the house would sell more easily if the garden was kept in good order. I'm so glad —"

"And now he's working for Grandmother."

Something stirred in Leonie's mind and gradually clarified.

"You used to play with his two children, didn't you?"

"Yes. They're still as delightful as ever. I saw them this evening."

"And Jim isn't married again?"

"No." Fran's brown eyes flicked to Leonie's face and away again. "He has managed somehow to bring those children up himself — he couldn't have done it, of course, if his job hadn't been on the spot. Gay is now nearly nine and Chris is seven. Jim still works part-time at Kew Gardens and he told me that they'd have him full-time directly he says the word, but he can't with two children to look after."

"He's good-looking and intelligent and kind — why on earth doesn't he find himself another wife?" Leonie protested. "Meg has been dead for years!"

"I — perhaps he will — one day —" Fran got up and went to the window. "You can just see his cottage from here, right up beyond the rhododendron hedge." She paused and then asked; "Do you remember, Leonie, how the police grilled him? It was cruel! It was horrible!"

"Everyone was questioned —"

"And Jim most of all — just because he was honest enough to admit to them that he had had a row the previous week with Marcus, and because he'd admitted to someone that he'd lost his temper and nearly hit him! As though everyone hadn't lost their temper with Marcus at some time or other and — and nearly hated him enough to wish him dead —" she swung from the window and put her hands to her face. "That's dreadful, saying that, isn't it? But it's true, Leonie!"

"Well, Jim was cleared. He was seen at the time of the murder working in one of the glass-houses at Kew.'"

"Yes —" Fran's eyes flicked to Leonie and slid away. "Yes, of course."

"So, he's got nothing to worry about. Nobody has, Fran, except the one who — who killed him."

A look of utter fear crossed Fran's face.

"Why talk as though there's a possibility of someone finding out who killed Marcus? Whoever did it must know he's safe by now. He *must* be! The police would have found the — the one who killed him if that person *could* be found!" She spoke defiantly.

"They seldom quite close a case —"

"That's what you said to Julian! Leonie, why are you bringing the whole thing to the surface again? *Why?* It does nobody any good! You just open closed doors — and —"

"They are already ajar," Leonie said. "If you weren't aware of the atmosphere in that room, *I* was! Marcus was uppermost in their thoughts, but they were daring anyone to mention him."

"We all want it forgotten except you! You're in an absolute minority here, Leonie! Look at this house, how everything's changed. And if you're haunted by memories you won't get any sympathy here! Grandmother intends to live here even if a thousand ghosts haunt it!"

"It was once her home, before she married and went to New Orleans, so I suppose it must be full of memories of her triumphs and they'd be much stronger for her than any thought of Marcus, whom she can scarcely have known."

"Then let it be that way, Leonie!" Fran urged. "Don't go trying to question and prove. I'm like the rest, I want it all buried deep, for ever!" She was trembling. "And I believe you would want it that way, too, if you'd ever known the other side of Marcus." She leaned for support against the light-panelled wall. "I believe whoever killed him suffered dreadfully – somehow – from him. I think he did whatever he did on a terrible impulse of such deep hurt that he was almost mad with it at the moment."

"I know Marcus could be cruel. But to *kill* –"

"You can't understand that, can you?" Fran's voice was quiet and despairing, "because you've never been hurt – not deeply in your heart so that you are blind with grief! But I – I –" she pushed her hands out in front of her. Her pretty features fought to control tears. She went half-blindly to the door and fumbled for the knob. "It's no use talking to you, Leonie!" Her voice shook. Then the door closed, and she was gone.

You've never been hurt – not deeply in your heart . . .

How little Fran knew! Or – how much?

Leonie went to the window. Somewhere down in that dark, beautiful garden with its silver patches and its sable shadows and its late spring scents, was Claire walking with Philip?

She leaned her head against the cool glass.

And suddenly she realised that, if they were there, they could see her, standing in her lighted room looking out. She shot away from the window, pulled the curtains and at the same time heard the curtains in the next room being drawn across the windows and realised that it was Fran's room.

Disturbed about the small scene with Fran, what puzzled her most was why she had been so upset tonight by the talk about Marcus. Had she been at one time one of the women who had loved him, secretly and blindly as so many had done? Had she been hurt by him: quarrelled with him and then, when he met his violent death did love rise again with regret and self-recrimination as so often happened after unexpected death. Was she haunted by some imaginary injustice she felt she had done him? Fran — and Marcus! If this were so, then the secret had been well kept!

She had not even considered such a thing a year ago and yet now, because she, Leonie, had forced them all to remember him, it seemed that secret emotions she had not dreamed about at the time surged to the surface. Were there angles in this case that not even the police dreamed about? Had Fran, the charming, the open-hearted, the frank, gone to join her parents in the Argentine in order to keep her secret safe from everyone?

But mere conjecture to-night, when she was tired, would only end in an uprush of violent imagination. Leonie looked across at her open suitcases and decided that action might stop thoughts that could lead nowhere.

While she unpacked, however, she wondered how thin was the door that shut Fran's secret from the world. Whatever it was, would she give herself away sooner or later — and would they all, herself included, bitterly regret the ghost she had resurrected in that great, glittering room to-night . . . ?

Carefully, she put her things away and stacked her suitcases in a corner. But she still felt too restless for bed.

She had managed to dismiss the memory of Fran for the more searing thought of Philip.

The discovery that he loved her was like a torch that burned inside her but could never be allowed to be held high before all the world. *Philip loves me and I love him . . . and it is too late!*

She heard the sound of a car being driven away and knew that he had gone. She felt the sound personally, as though he had just taken leave of her — she could almost imagine that he had kissed her good-bye; her lips felt warm with the imagined touch!

There was a soft, dragging footstep on the stairs. Leonie stood quite still, head turned towards the door, listening to it, wondering what Claire and Philip had had to say to one another out there in the garden where she had left them. She heard the footsteps pass her door, move on down the passage. Then a door opened and closed in the distance and the house was silent again.

Without knowing what she intended to do, Leonie opened her own door quietly and went to the head of the stairs. A dim light burned in the hall. She found herself going downstairs, moving automatically along the corridor to the back of the house, her feet silent on the new red carpet. Then, at the closed door, she paused.

Her hand was on the cool, painted-china handle and before she was strengthened for the ordeal, her fingers had taken command and turned the knob. The door swung open.

She was standing on the threshold of the room in which Marcus had died.

Moonlight gave the scene a flat picture-like quality and took the clear, bright yellow from the curtains.

Leonie turned and switched on the light and the room sprang to life, with colour and perspective.

She saw, then, that this was the one room in the house that had not been changed at all. Not, she was certain, because there was any sentiment in old Venetia, but probably because she had not yet quite the courage to face the room and direct its alterations.

"It's never wise to recall tragedy, Leonie! I thought I told you that."

She swung round. Venetia stood there. She wore a dressing-gown of black-tulip silk and she looked very much older with her hair no longer piled on top of her head.

"I heard someone down here," she said and walked into the room. "I wondered if it were you. Why do you want to see this room?"

"I don't know," Leonie said honestly. "I had to come down — it wasn't just a sort of ghoulish inquisitiveness — I don't think I really wanted to come —" she broke off, unable to explain.

The old eyes watched her. "Did you speak the truth when you said that you weren't going to marry Marcus?"

"Yes."

Venetia smiled. "You didn't know it, Leonie, but I had an idea when your parents died, to have you out in the States with me. Marcus, however, got you. He was delighted with you."

Leonie leaned slightly against the desk. "Was he?" her tone was flat.

"Do you like Julian?"

The question was so unexpected that for a moment Leonie didn't answer. Then she said, cautiously, "I can't really tell. I haven't had time to know him."

"First impressions are very important."

"I suppose so. But I like to get to know people before I really make up my mind —"

"You *will* like Julian. He's charming and talented and you share the same interests. When you stood talking to him earlier this evening, I watched you and I thought : 'If only he had met her first!' "

Leonie made a startled, involuntary movement, reaching out her hand, and her fingers touched the grey stone cat, back now in its place on the desk. Her arm shot away as though her hand had been burned. She stared at Venetia, not quite believing that she understood.

"Hilda has *nothing* to give Julian," old Venetia continued.

"Except her love for him! That's important, Grandmother."

"Hilda never loved Julian — she just wanted him!" her grandmother said clearly. "She was getting on, she's six years older than

Julian, and so *she* married *him*. It was done before I had a chance to stop it." She paused and closed her eyes for a moment. Then opening them very wide, she added. "It won't last, Leonie. It can't — *it mustn't be allowed to!*"

"Sometimes it takes time for two people to grow together," Leonie said, swift to Hilda's defence.

"But I don't *want* them to grow together," she said almost pettishly. Then she laid a thin hand on Leonie's arm and her manner became both confiding and imperious. "Julian will get somewhere in the theatre world if he has a strong woman by his side. Hilda is a clinger; she'll keep him back!" She drew a long breath. "Get to know Julian, Leonie. *Like* him!"

"But I — I'm sure I will!"

"Like him a very great deal, because I have plans for you both — together."

Her meaning was too obvious to be ignored. The conversation had become hateful.

"I don't want anyone to have plans for me," she said coldly. "I want to work out my own."

"Of course you do, child, but perhaps you will find that yours and mine are the same. Julian — oh well, never mind now. There's plenty of time." She smiled to herself, nodding faintly, and changed the subject. "I am keeping this door locked now that there are people in the house. I don't want to find imaginative nervy little fools like Hilda wandering in here and getting hysterical. We don't need to use this room for the time being, anyway."

There was a question Leonie had to ask. She walked towards the door.

"Do you mind living in this house, Grandmother? I mean — because of Marcus?"

"Why should I? I scarcely knew him." Her eyes flicked to the piano, the desk, the curtains that had made a back-cloth for his body a year ago. "If I'd minded all the things that happened to me in my life, my dear girl, I'd be a nervous wreck!"

"Who *could* have done it?" Leonie whispered.

"You must stop harping on that, Leonie! If it helps, why don't you look on it as, perhaps, an accident?"

"Then why didn't someone come forward and say so?"

Venetia made an impatient gesture. "Would anyone admit to murder — or at best, to manslaughter? If any of us had a chance to escape, we'd escape. I would — and so would you if the situation ever arose! Marcus made many enemies. Perhaps one of the musicians he sacked came back and quarrelled with him; perhaps his agent, or his music publisher, or his gardener of his housekeeper killed him. You may even include Philip – or Claire –"

"There are people it couldn't possibly have been. Florrie and Philip – and Claire, since she didn't even know him."

The paper-thin lids closed over the old eyes.

"In murder, you can leave no one out! If I were conjecturing, I would even include you, Leonie! Don't look so shocked. I'm merely trying to show you that it will help no one to start probing. Old wounds must be left to heal. And now, let's go to bed."

She locked the door carefully and pocketed the key.

They went upstairs in silence, Leonie walking behind the slow, rustling figure of her grandmother.

But, lying in the big bed, Leonie neither slept nor remembered. She was trying to find a reason that would be acceptable to old Venetia for leaving Heron House.

One by one they came, and were dismissed. Probably her brain was tired; probably too much energy had been used for one evening. The fact remained, she could find no valid reason for going away as soon as she arrived. And she could not tell her grandmother the truth. She could not say:

"Marcus played a cruel trick on Philip and me. We love one another and I can't stay in the house with the girl he is going to marry!" She did not know her grandmother well enough to trust her with such a secret. And besides the matter of love, there was a sensation that the house itself held her prisoner, as though its old walls taunted because they knew the truth, holding it in their aged, inanimate bones.

IV

Leonie breakfasted in bed the next morning. Boadicea brought it up on a pink tray with water-lilies painted on it.

When she had bathed and dressed, Leonie went downstairs to find the house quiet except for Hilda, bustling about with a duster, singing little snatches of song as though to pretend all was right with her world. How strange, Leonie thought, to hear Hilda's thin, high voice wobbling through the rooms instead of the rich, flowing tones of Marcus's piano! Marcus, playing Beethoven and lifting one up, making one forget one's anger with him for some outrageous thing he had said or done, because of the throbbing beauty of the music. Marcus playing Brahms, Scarlatti; playing Bach's "Sheep May Safely Graze" as though his whole being were transcendental, seeing God and the highest heaven!

It was all so vivid that Leonie turned and went quickly out into the garden.

Spring had stolen summer's weather and the

sky was like stretched silk of softest blue.

Beyond the vegatable garden and the bank of pink rhododendrons was the gardener's cottage. Turning towards it in search of Jim Farraday, she could see the push and thrust of his spade working in the small walled lupin garden. She went far enough forward to be able to see him clearly. The sun shone on to his nearly black hair and his strong body had a masculine grace as it moved.

At the time the police had come to question them all, Jim had told them that the quarrel he had had with Marcus some weeks earlier had been over work in the garden. It had struck Leonie then as strange because never in all the years he had been working at Heron House had there been the slightest difference of opinion between them regarding the planting and planning of that acre. *Had* that been the reason for their quarrel? She remembered Fran's scared look the night before, how she had cried that it was horrible the way the police had "grilled" him; how she had demanded: "Why keep on about who killed Marcus? . . . I want it all buried deep and for ever . . . !" Why? Because she knew something she wanted to forget? Had she, Leonie asked herself, been wrong in linking Fran's name with Marcus? Refreshed after her sleep, her mind no longer seized upon the obvious. Now she asked herself whether Fran knew something about that quarrel Jim had had with Marcus! If that was it, then why did she want to defend him so violently?

Leonie watched him straighten up and stand for a moment, leaning on his spade, looking away over the slope of the hill towards the Thames and the green fields.

"Leonie! Come and see what I'm doing."

She started at Julian's voice from somewhere down the path, and moved her head, looking for him. He was standing at the door of the summer-house down near the back gate. It had a rush roof and wooden walls and although Marcus never used it, it had always been kept in good repair. As a child, Leonie had played there. As a young girl she used to escape there to control some anger or fight some hurt Marcus had dealt her.

Behind the summer-house was an old wall that was the boundary of the garden and beyond it was the little lower road that led to nowhere very much.

He was waiting for her, standing in the doorway.

"I've got all my bits and pieces in here," he said, "I want to show them to you," and stood aside for Leonie to enter.

The sun poured through the windows on to tables laden with paints and carpenters' tools. A small model theatre stood on a stand near the door and all around were minute pieces of furniture, little painted stage sets and tiny dolls. The place was in a state of utter disorder and there was a feeling of vivid activity here. Julian saw her gaze move to the floor which was strewn with bits of wood, paint and cigarette ends.

"Nobody comes in here to clean," he explained. "I just don't allow it. Venetia thinks it's all quite horrible, but she gives in to me *over this.*" The last two words had emphasis. "I think even she realises that I've got to have somewhere which can be really mine and only mine!"

To Leonie there was almost the smell of the theatre about it. It was a strange, exciting, not particularly pleasant smell that quickened the blood of those whose lives were spent in the theatre.

She went up to one of the tables.

Julian followed her. "This," he indicated the toy stage, "is being planned for a new play Ross Menara is putting on at the Alex Theatre. It's very modern and there have to be three rooms seen at the same time. Menara suggested that I might like to try my hand, and if he approves the result, then I shall work on it."

"You did stage design work in the States, didn't you?" she asked, regarding him with interest.

He nodded. "And I have introductions to people over here."

It was fascinating to watch him as he showed her what he was doing; his fingers moved delicately among the tiny pieces; a cow-lick of waving, straw-coloured hair fell over his forehead; the weakness of his mouth was transformed into charm by his slight, absorbed smile.

"I always work with a little stage; it makes me feel part of the set I'm planning," he looked at her over his shoulder. "Tell me about yourself, Leonie."

She perched on the end of a table and found it easy to talk theatre to him. And gradually she realised, as Julian talked too, how parallel their lives had been. Brought up by ambitious people; trained to appreciate beautiful things; strangers to real affection, to warmth and belonging — they might have been moulded in the same clay. Leonie tried to talk about Hilda, but he dismissed her in monosyllables. To her husband, also, Hilda had become "Julian's Folly"!

Leonie was nearly late for rehearsals that

morning. She dashed on to the stage just as the cast was sorting itself out.

Whenever she was acting, nothing else existed. She moved, absorbed and uplifted, through the exhausting day and when she left the rehearsal, the words of the play and the story of which she was part, wrapped her round in a cocoon.

Only that evening when she walked up the drive of the house on Richmond Hill again, did she emerge from one world into the other.

The fine Georgian house stood in solid grace and the dying saffron and eau-de-nil light from the sky fell on to the fine portico so that it seemed that it was about to burst into living bloom.

Above her the trees whispered; her footsteps crunched on the drive and those were the only sounds save for those, distant and seemingly unreal, of the traffic on Richmond Hill. She had felt even in the old days of living here that once she turned in at the drive, she moved in an enclosed world. The traffic and the people became the dream and only Marcus's house was the reality. And so strong was his personality that even now, a year after his death, the same sensation of enclosure swept her as she walked towards the house.

Lights were on in some of the rooms and, as

she let herself in, Boadicea came from the kitchen and told her that Venetia had gone to bed.

"Miss Fran am out somewhere; Miss Claire am in her room. Mr. Julian, he am way down de garden, workin'. M's Hilda —" she shrugged her massive shoulders. "I dunno!"

The door closed and Boadicea hovered.

"You like somept'in', M's Sarat?"

Leonie considered the question, saw the time by the ornate Louis Quinze clock over the great hall fireplace and said:

"Were you watching television, Boadicea?"

"Yes Ma'am," she beamed.

"Well, you go back to it. If I want anything I'll get it myself."

"You sur', Mis' Sarat?" She showed her splendid white teeth, and then, as Leonie reassured her, she bounced off with a swing of a candy-striped dress.

There was no reason to break herself of the old habit of drinking tea late at night just because she was not in her own flat. Leonie went into the kitchen.

Gone was the clinical whiteness of Florrie's domain. Now it was a riot of yellow and green and red, like a barrow-load of fruit. Leonie suspected that Venetia had allowed Boadicea to have her way in this, which was her world, and the negress had taken full advantage of the opportunity.

In the adjoining pantry were all Venetia's beautiful china and glass. Leonie went to the dresser and took down a homely pink cup and saucer and found a pink and brown earthenware teapot on a shelf.

When the tea was made, she poured herself out a cup and sat down at the big kitchen table, drawing towards her a cookery book. Opening it, she saw Boadicea's heavy markings against words needed to describe parts of animals — and remembered that the various "cuts" of meat were different in the States.

"Leonie!"

Her name was spoken so quietly that she started almost guiltily.

"Oh, hallo Hilda! I've just made some tea — come and have a cup — or haven't you got the English habit yet?"

Julian's wife wore a dark red housecoat. She padded across the kitchen in her flat-heeled velvet slippers and reached for a cup and saucer. "I'm so tired," she said and sat down heavily in a chair.

"What have you been doing?"

"Oh nothing. Perhaps that's the reason! I took Julian's car this evening and drove myself around. I often do, you know, it's better than sitting alone."

"Do you need to be alone?"

"Unless Venetia is around to talk theatre to him, Julian spends most of his time in what he calls his Studio." Her voice, with its slow Southern drawl, lacked vitality. Something was draining her, something more than mere boredom.

Hilda lifted her cup and then put it down again.

"I wish I'd never come here!" her voice was violent.

"Don't you like England?"

"I guess England's all right, but I hate this house. And now, it seems, we're here for — for as long as Venetia lives!"

"If Julian makes a success of stage designing, you'll be able to have a home of your own."

"As though Venetia would ever let that happen! She's got him! She's got us both!"

"But you could probably talk to her and make her see how you feel," Leonie urged. "You're both young, you need to lead your own lives."

"You think anything I could say would move her one little inch?" she gulped her tea without enjoyment.

"Things change. You never know. Perhaps one day —"

"Things change," Hilda said vehemently. "People die — they *do* die, don't they, Leonie? No one lives for ever!"

Leonie would not meet those desperate eyes. She traced the line of the painted flowers on the teapot, feeling it hot to her finger. *One day, Venetia would die. . . . and then —*

"Just wait till Julian really gets established," Leonie said. "He'll probably want a home of his own," she glanced covertly at Hilda. "When I was a little girl," she rushed on trying to take her mind off her unhappiness, "I used to spend a lot of my time in this kitchen. Florrie was Marcus's housekeeper and she used to show me how to make toffee. She was Scottish and very kind. In the evening she used to sit here and play patience and cheat. She has retired now and gone back to Thurso to live with her two sisters. It's a beautiful, light kitchen, isn't it?"

But Hilda wasn't listening. She sat tensely, following the train of her own thoughts.

"I've no one here to talk to about it."

"About what?"

Hilda pushed back her hair and it stood up like little blonde sprigs. "Why, this house. You see, I *know* something awful is going to happen if we stay!"

"But it's a perfectly ordinary house," Leonie

said firmly, "with ordinary people in it — if you discount Grandmother. Though after all, she's just an old lady now with a wonderful past! Nothing awful is going to happen here. Just because someone you never knew died violently —"

"But you don't understand! Leonie, what can I *do?* I must talk to someone. I shall go mad if I don't."

"I shouldn't do that if I were you!" Leonie said lightly.

Hilda pushed her cup away violently and some of the tea spilled in the saucer. Leonie reached out and gripped her arm.

"If you've got something to say, Hilda, say it! Don't hint."

"Now *you're* angry with me! Leonie, don't be, because I *am* scared. This house; that room where Marcus died. You feel it too! You said so last night, and it made them angry. Even Philip — I watched him. You see, I believe they all know that something is going to happen. Someone, Leonie, is watching, waiting —"

In one minute, Leonie thought, I'm going to have to slap her because she'll get hysterical!

Hilda's hand gripped the edge of the table. Her eyes were closed, her housecoat had fallen apart to reveal her plump little neck and shoulders.

"Hilda!" Leonie reached out and shook her hard.

"I'm sorry." She opened her eyes. "I'm being the sort of fool they always expect me to be! But it's terribly serious, really it is. You see — I'm — in — danger!"

"What danger?"

"If I tell you, will you give me your absolute promise not to repeat anything I say?"

"No, if it's really serious, I certainly won't."

"But you must. You see, what I know could hurt you, too! You're in danger as well, Leonie."

Perhaps she should have laughed and broken the tension, but for the life of her she couldn't! Hilda was in deadly earnest and what she said and the way she said it was far too stark to be tossed aside as a neurotic outburst.

"How can I possibly be in danger," Leonie asked as lightly as she could. "Come to that, how can *you?*"

"I know who killed Marcus."

Now I know she's just a mixed-up hysteric, Leonie thought.

"Please believe me," Hilda was pleading. "I'm not making it up. I'm not brave enough to enjoy saying frightening things."

"How can you know? And if you do —"

"I can't tell you any more. It's enough, isn't

it, to know that you're in danger and so am I."

"The more you tell me so that it is no longer just *your* secret, the safer you'll be," Leonie said, humouring her. "Who?"

"Don't ask!"

"Then tell me why I'm in danger, surely I have a right to know that!"

"You don't realise that you know something that could incriminate someone. But if you start questioning and probing, you may — find out. That's why," she was shivering.

"But Hilda," Leonie said as quietly as she could, "I told the police all I knew."

"All you thought you knew *then!* But someone in this house is frightened of you — and if you show too much interest —" she broke off, put both her hands round her cup and tried to drink, slopping it. "It makes it easier, though, if I feel someone else knows, too —"

"But I *don't* know! You haven't told me. You've just made an incredible statement and then left it in the air! How do you know who killed Marcus?"

"I —" Hilda began and then set her lips in a tight, stubborn line.

"If you won't tell me, then you must tell the police."

"I wouldn't be allowed to — I wouldn't

be alive long enough—"

"Oh, really," Leonie said with sudden impatience, hiding her own alarm, "now you're making it all pure melodrama!"

"Melodrama happens! You can read it any day in the newspapers — so why shouldn't it happen to us? Someone has come to this house, Leonie, who —" she broke off, lifted her head and whispered. "Who's that?"

"No one."

Hilda turned. "Leonie, please, oh, please don't start asking more questions, don't go around here talking as you did last night. I thought — if I told you what I did, you'd see how — how dangerous it was and leave the past alone."

This time there *was* a sound. Julian called Hilda from the hall. She started up and, without looking round, fled to him.

Leonie was only vaguely aware of her going with the swift slip-slap of her slippers. She sat quite still, staring down at the table and telling herself that Venetia was right and Hilda was a little fool. A dangerous little fool, if one let oneself be identified with her hysterics. . . .

And then came Julian's voice again:

"For heaven's sake, you'll be fit for nothing tomorrow if you don't go to bed!"

Claire's voice called from somewhere on the stairs:

"Oh, Julian, I'm looking for my library book. Is it on the hall table? Or I might have left it in the car."

Julian in the hall; Claire on the stairs. . . . Someone waiting . . . someone listening. . . . And Hilda, in her carrying Southern States voice, saying: "I know who killed Marcus" . . . And Philip loving her — and Claire standing between them. . . .

V

"Have you seen my library book?"

Leonie, carrying cups to the kitchen sink, looked over her shoulder and saw Claire.

"No."

"I thought I'd left it on the hall table," she came limping into the kitchen, "but if it's still in the car, I really can't be bothered to get it. Or Fran could have taken it by mistake. She was wandering around with a red-covered book under her arm. I saw her just before she went down to the cottage."

"You mean Jim's cottage?"

"Of course." Claire's lids lifted and dropped again over her eyes with a small, sly movement. "She goes down there a lot. Well, he's a handsome man."

Her inference was clear.

"Fran has known Jim for years," Leonie said defensively. "She used to come here in – in the old days."

"Yes I'm sure she did! She knew Marcus very well, didn't she?"

"She was a cousin —"

"And she got ill, didn't she, after Marcus was killed." Claire was smiling, very faintly. "I wonder what upset her so?"

For a moment Leonie looked at her without answering. *I do dislike her so! But it isn't just because of Philip. . . .*

Claire was waiting for her to speak. Leonie turned her gaze away. She was strong and she had a will of her own. But Claire was stronger — and subtle and secretive! Softly she urged:

"Do *you* know what made Fran suddenly leave England?"

"She had been over-working at the Youth Hostel. Then she got 'flu and got up before she should have done. The doctor ordered her away and she went down for a week or two to stay with an old servant for whom Fran's father had bought a charming cottage in the country as compensation for not taking her with them to the Argentine."

"Fran was ill and went down there after Marcus's death. Yes, I heard about that. And then she slipped out of the country —"

"To stay with her people outside Buenos Aires. It had always been an accepted thing that she would visit them as soon as they got settled."

Claire smiled. "And after Marcus died,

the moment was opportune?"

"What do you mean?" she was aware of the sharp enmity in her voice.

But it did not trouble Claire.

"Why, before Marcus's death, Fran was down here quite a bit, wasn't she? And —"

"And — *what?*"

"Oh — nothing!" Her voice indicated that what she was thinking was anything but unimportant.

"You've said so much, I think you'd better tell me the rest."

"There's nothing actually that *I* can tell — I only conjecture. After all, why shouldn't Fran be friends with Jim if she wants to? Though I guess Marcus had plenty to say if he ever knew about that friendship in the old days — and from what I've heard of Marcus I'm certain that he knew! There'd have been quite a scene!" The slow smile was still on her face. "In fact the second act of a drama! 'Marcus Sarat Has His Say! The Reactions of Two Young People. Angry Words. Threats! *Curtain!*'"

Leonie had begun to rinse the two cups under the tap. Now she stopped and lifted her head slightly.

"Are you trying to infer that Fran used to come down here to see Jim and not Marcus?"

"My dear Leonie, how should *I* know! I wasn't part of the scene in those days. Only, I read the newspapers and I heard people talk and – well, face it, Leonie! *You* knew Marcus, so you must realise the sort of reaction there'd have been if he had ever thought his cousin was getting interested in his gardener!"

"I think we won't discuss it!"

"Very well, I'm sure I don't care what Fran does. I scarcely know her! Only, since I'm in this house where so much took place, naturally I'm curious. Unsolved mysteries are like unfinished cross-words – you can't rest until you know all the answers." She limped across the room. "Have you been having tea?"

"Yes."

"Is there any left?"

"We've drained the pot. But you can make some more."

"I won't bother. I'm tired –" her voice took on a plaintive little sound. "My leg has been hurting me this evening. I've been standing too much –"

"Sit down then and I'll make you some fresh tea."

"No! I'll have some milk if there's any to spare."

"Heaps." Leonie went to the refrigerator and poured out a glass.

Claire took it and stood with it in her hands. Her green quilted taffeta housecoat made her look like a little girl. She was so small and so fragile-looking. Only her eyes had no child's innocence.

"It must be strange coming back here." She was watching Leonie over the rim of her glass.

"It is."

Leonie turned off the taps and wiped the cups. *Go! Go! Go!* But Claire was all set for a talk and there was a curious strength in her that commanded a hearing. She was like a tiny, lethal weapon, Leonie thought and wondered why she disliked her so.

"Such a lovely house — so perfect in its period. I wish I could be given the job of redecorating it. The things in it, the furniture and the colouring don't 'go.' "

"It was different in Marcus's time." She glanced at Claire casually as she passed her on the way to empty the tea-pot. The lids were lowered so that her lashes made dark smudges on her cheek.

"I believe," Claire said, "that Marcus had perfect taste. Philip told me." She drank some of her milk. "It's terrible that such a lovely old house should have this cloud over it now, isn't it."

"I suppose all old houses have some cloud or

other," Leonie said evasively. "You can't expect generations of people who have lived in them to have been without tragedy."

"But murder!" she sighed, "and you were here when it happened — the newspaper said so. Leonie, didn't you have the slightest suspicion who did it?"

"If I had, I'd have told the police."

"You might not!"

Leonie turned; her hands, wiping the teapot, slowed in their movements.

"Why wouldn't I?"

"Loyalty, for instance."

"If you were faced with police questions, I don't believe you'd find it easy to evade honest answers — even if you wanted to!"

"I suppose not, but with a man like Marcus — so brilliant, so curiously attractive —"

"You knew him?" Leonie heard her voice rapping her question out over the quiet kitchen.

Claire smiled. "I saw him conducting orchestras lots of times — I've always loved music. And one day I saw him here. Philip had to bring some papers out on a Saturday afternoon — I remember my father saying about the Sarats, that the day and the hour was unimportant; if they wanted something at midnight on Christmas Day, they'd see they got it!" She leaned a little against the table. "We were going into the country that afternoon, Philip and I, and when he left me in the car I began thinking how I'd love to see inside that house. And then Marcus came to the door with Philip and opened it wide. I saw, then, those heavenly carpets on the wall, glowing like pieces of velvet, and the great bowl of flowers on the table."

Leonie put the tea-pot back on the dresser.

"I suppose," Claire went on, "the police questioned everyone."

"Everyone!" Leonie said bitterly. "Me, most of all!"

"You? But you must have been the last person to be suspected. I mean, Marcus was so good to you, and you adored him, didn't you?"

"No. I was grateful to him and I admired him."

"I was engaged to Philip at the time. But I saw a lot of him and I made him tell me about it — after all, my father's firm *were* the Sarat lawyers, so I felt I had an almost personal interest. Of course, Marcus had masses of acquaintances so that the field of suspects was large. You knew all his friends?"

"No. I hadn't been living in this house for a long time before it happened."

"Marcus must have talked to you about the

people he knew?" she insisted.

"He didn't. Not much! He was a secretive person when he chose."

"But you and Fran used to come here so often — you must have known his friends — suspected — *someone?*"

"I suspected no one I knew."

"You mean you had an idea that someone you didn't know —"

"I suspected no one!" Leonie cut in.

Claire was unmoved by the violent exasperation in her voice.

"When you left Heron House," she continued, "and started to live on your own, I remember Father telling me that he wouldn't be surprised if Marcus offered Fran a home here."

"But she had her job and she loved it!"

"Oh, I know. But a girl wouldn't be human who didn't jump at the chance to live in luxury here. She'd think probably that nothing that Marcus could do or say could spoil such a glamorous style of living. I know *you* walked out — but I suppose you're one of those dedicated people. Do you think Fran was asked to come here and then somehow blotted her copybook and there was a row with Marcus? Do you think? —" Claire broke off. "Oh well, perhaps I'd better not say any more."

"I shouldn't," Leonie said shortly, and for a moment silenced Claire.

What was she trying to find out? She was shooting questions like a detective, probing and pressing her points. Fran and Marcus . . . or Fran and Jim Farraday?

Leonie said briskly:

"Look, Claire, I know nothing! I wish I did. But I'd really rather not talk about it any more to-night. I've had a long day and I'm going to bed. Turn the lights out, won't you?"

"You don't like talking about Marcus, do you?" the smile at her mouth didn't reach her eyes. "I'm sorry. I suppose you think I'm very curious."

But she wasn't in the least bit sorry and she *was* very curious!

"Good night, Claire."

Leonie left her standing there alone in the enormous kitchen. She was drinking her milk like a little girl, both hands held round the glass. A little girl? A young woman with a great artistic gift, an inexhaustible curiosity and a capacity for violence kept locked in her slender limping body.

Walking up the curved staircase to her room, Leonie wondered about that curiosity of Claire's. Was it merely that murder – if you weren't directly involved – had a macabre fascination? But there had been that in Claire's manner that spoke of something deeper than mere curiosity, and something in what she had said that troubled Leonie vaguely.

She tried to think back to what it was that hadn't rung true in their conversation, but the memory was blurred and only the sensation remained.

Leonie walked to her window, pulled back the curtains and stared out at the dark garden. Other thoughts crowded Claire out, even more troubling, more sinister.

I know who killed Marcus!

She could tell herself that it was merely a flight of Hilda's imagination, but she didn't really believe that. Hilda knew something — and because she had promised, Leonie could say nothing to anyone about it. . . .

Or could she be expected to hold on to such a promise in a matter so serious? Should she tell Philip? But he would say: "Go to the police." And if she did, would Hilda deny, when she was being questioned, that she had said any such thing? If it were true that she thought her knowledge was a danger to herself, she would probably protest that the whole thing was a fabrication. The police might then conclude that the conversation had been thought up by Leonie in order to attract attention to herself.

An actress seeking publicity anyhow, anywhere – as long as she got it!

Stop letting it get you down! Old Venetia was right. Hilda was a hysteric and Leonie began to see why her grandmother had resented Julian's marriage.

Yet, even while she tried to lull her emotions, the nagging memory remained of Hilda's eyes, most deeply and genuinely frightened. . . .

VI

The following morning, the sunlight and the birds' songs dispersed the fears of the previous night.

Leonie took her breakfast tray into the kitchen and stood talking to Boadicea for a while, interested to know how she liked England.

The kindly negress had been out very little. She seemed to be perfectly happy as long as she had her bright kitchen, her television, and her "M's Venetia" to love and gently bully.

Later, on the sunny terrace, Leonie met Hilda. She wore a blue cotton dress and her hair was brushed back in a kind of practical "morning chores" neatness. She had put on her rouge in two bright dollops, like a Dutch doll. She should have been pretty, but her obsession with fear made her careless with her appearance and she was like a woman who knew nobody ever really looked at her with interest any more.

"Oh Leonie —" her gaze darted round and

then, reassured that no one was within earshot, she went on. "I'm sorry about last night, I don't know what was the matter with me, but please forget it!"

"You can't expect me to do that!"

"But you see, I'm sure I was mistaken. I get nervy in this house — everything here is so different from home and, well, I just got to imagining. Venetia always says I'm an awful fool." She was watching Leonie's face anxiously. "So you won't repeat what I told you, will you?"

Leonie knew that her own expression was uncompromising; Hilda rushed on:

"I don't know anything — really I don't! How could I? I just got to — sort of — pretending that I knew things — working myself up into a state just because I don't like it here —" Her eyes went beyond Leonie and her body tensed. A false little smile wreathed her face: "Oh hallo, Claire? Just off to work?"

"Yes, and I may be back late. Would you ask Boadicea to leave me something cold, please? Not much because I'm a small eater."

She moved away towards her car and Julian joined them from the house. He wore brown corduroys and a blue shirt and he looked handsome and a little dishevelled. Turning to Hilda, Leonie found that she was no longer there. She was darting across the lawn after her little white cat, Livvy.

"I had a letter this morning from Ross Menara," Julian was saying. "He likes my sketches for the sets and I'm going up to see him this morning."

"That's wonderful, Julian. I'm so glad! Have you told Grandmother? She'll be pleased, too." (*And do you know what your wife said to me last night? I wish I could tell you . . . I wish I could tell someone. . . .*)

Julian was saying:

"When Venetia read the letter, all she said was, 'Well, if you can't act, I suppose this is the next best thing!' And then she told me to talk it over with you; she said we'd be able to help each other, you and I."

A tradesman coming up the drive caught Leonie's attention, and she turned and smiled a "Good morning" to him.

Julian was glancing at his watch.

"I'll be going to town in a little while. Perhaps I could give you a lift?"

"Thank you. I've got a rehearsal this morning."

"In about ten minutes, then?"

"Leonie!" a clear, carrying voice called her. "Will you please go and tell those screaming children to be quiet. This is a private garden

104

not the bear house at the zoo." Venetia stood just down the path, holding an overblown red tulip. "If Jim is playing with his children you can tell him he'd be better employed clearing the flower beds."

"He's working in the vegetable garden. I saw him just now."

"Then on your way to stop those children behaving like animals, you'll please tell him I want to see him."

Erect as a queen, she turned and walked away and Leonie became suddenly aware of the children's laughter and cries of delight – but certainly no screaming.

She found Jim and he anchored his spade into the earth and looked at her with delight out of blue eyes.

"Miss Leonie! Well, it is good to see you!"

"I meant to come and see you yesterday morning, but I got waylaid." She held out her hand.

"I'm grubby," he said hesitantly.

"God's good earth!" she laughed and took his hand firmly. "I've been sent to say my grand-mother would like to see you. But sometime we've got to have a talk – it's so long since I've seen you, and I want to know all about the children and what new and wonderful things you're managing to grow at Kew."

"I've seen *you* – on television. The children remember you, too –" he listened to their laughter. "I believe Fran's with them."

So she was "Fran" to him! Remembering her errand for Venetia, she said hastily, "I'm here for a month, so we'll be meeting." She walked quickly away towards the cottage, a small brown house behind flowering rhododendrons. Two children, as fair as Meg Farraday had been, were fighting for a large red ball. On the patch of lawn sat Fran, tousled and laughing, her full yellow skirt like a gigantic daffodil against the green of the new grass.

The children saw Leonie first. They paused and stared curiously at her. Fran turned her brown head.

"Oh hallo. You all know one another, don't you? Leonie, this is Gay. Hasn't she grown?"

The stares vanished. They smiled politely and remotely. She had been away from them for over a year and that was a long time to small memories. Jim had said they'd seen her on television, but that was another world to them.

Leonie crossed the small lawn.

"You've both grown so much since I last saw you. I like your short hair Gay, and Chris – my –! you're going to be as tall as your father when you grow up!"

Their eyes never left her face.

Fran said: "Don't you remember when the four of us went for a picnic down by the river and, Gay, you found a scarlet pimpernel?"

"That reminds me," Leonie went on smoothly. "Do you both still have a patch of garden for your own?"

That thawed the ice. They rushed to show her their plots. Gay grew tulips, red and yellow, and pansies and old-fashioned nasturtiums. Chris had a mania for putting fruit pips into the soil. In spite of his father's warnings that nothing would come up, something did. Little bursts of green sprouted through the rich soil. His pride, however, was his chicory which his father had started for him. He had, he explained, two budgerigars and they liked chicory. Would Miss Leonie like to see them?

"I'm just off to work, but you must show them to me some other time." She motioned to Fran who rose from the grass with a swirl of yellow skirt. "Grandmother really sent me," she continued in a low voice, "because she says the children are making too much noise."

Fran's eyes flashed.

"They're playing far more quietly than most children!"

"Maybe they are, but —"

"But our grandmother wants to remind us that this is her house! I know! For heaven's sake, she can't hear much all that way away. What's her next move? Is she going to stop the traffic going up Richmond Hill? " 'The Queen is Displeased!' " she mocked, but there was anger in her eyes.

"I suppose they'll be at school most of the day," Leonie said, "so she won't have them here very much except at week-ends."

"Why didn't you tell her when she complained, that children can't be expected to speak in whispers?" Fran turned on Leonie. "Or perhaps it doesn't matter to you whether Jim's children are happy or not!"

"Hey!" Leonie protested. "I'm only a carrier of messages! Don't blame me!"

"I'm sorry," the violence went out of Fran. She shrugged her shoulders. "I'm touchy over Jim's children. Hang it all, they haven't got a mother, and he's brought them up jolly well. They're not rowdy and this is their garden, why should Grandmother interfere? Oh, all right, I'll keep them quiet!" she turned. "Gay, Chris — let's go down to the river, and we'll find somewhere where we can all have ice-cream sodas."

But walking back down the path to rejoin Julian, Leonie was troubled. Very rarely, in the past, Fran's charm had been shattered by violent anger – usually justified. She knew how her temper could devastate others and exhaust herself and she kept it in admirable control. But here was something which would be fuel to the flame of her anger – the effort to frustrate Jim's children in their play. Fran loved all young things and, with no job at the moment, Gay and Chris would have all her attention.

Leonie paused and saw, through the gap in the yew hedge, Jim working again in the vegetable garden. He had obviously had his interview with Venetia and it had been brief. He seemed to feel her gaze and straightened himself and turned. But there was no smile, no serenity on his face. He looked like a man digging a blazing temper out of his system.

First Fran and now Jim! Old Venetia and her lordly ways was going to throw many spanners into the works here in this house which had, in Marcus's time, run so smoothly!

Leonie felt her own impartial observation and, as looker-on, could imagine and understand both sides. Venetia was intending to over-see Jim's work, but he was too expert and independent a gardener to be taken from the job he felt the most important, to attend to some small task his employer chose to order him to do. Marcus had given him free rein and he had never abused that. On the other hand, Venetia was old and all her life she had been obeyed; she was temperamental and autocratic and it would be impossible to expect her to change now, at over eighty. Perhaps things would settle down. At any rate they were all adults and must cope with their own difficulties.

Julian was waiting for her by his car. Leonie flung the coat she had fetched over her shoulders and got into the passenger seat.

Driving with Julian was a nerve-racking business. At the third narrow escape from a collision, he said:

"I don't usually drive as badly as this. My mind isn't on my driving this morning; there's so much we have to talk about, Leonie. Venetia's right. It *is* wonderful for me to have you — she said it would be; she said she had great plans for us both!"

It was probably nothing, but listening, Leonie felt disturbed. She must be strong in dealing with old Venetia's machinations. Any seed she might choose to stimulate must fall on fallow ground; nothing, neither sympathy nor understanding between them, must water that seed. Anyway, how could it? Julian was married and Philip was in her heart and there was no room for any other man. . . .

After rehearsals that day, Leonie had to appear in a television play. She had therefore planned to stay quietly in her flat before going to the Television Studios.

She poached herself an egg, unwrapped some cream cheese and sat in front of a small fire, lit more for its cheerfulness than because she needed warmth. She had put on a blue silk housecoat and blue wedge sandals. Here, in the quiet, familiar atmosphere of her own small flat, the fears and tensions of Heron House were like the nightmares of dis-oriented people. She could even bring herself to be a little amused at the atmosphere an old tragedy could conjure up for those, including herself, receptive enough to be influenced twelve whole months later.

She had finished her meal when the doorbell rang.

For a moment she stood still, deciding to let it ring and then, when it pealed again, she went reluctantly into the hall.

Last time it had rung, Philip had stood outside.

This time, as she opened the door, it was as though time were telescoped. Philip again stood there. . . .

He saw her quick surprise and an expression of doubt crossed his face.

"You are expecting me, aren't you?"

"No. But come in."

"Isn't Hilda here yet?"

"Hilda?"

He entered the living-room explaining:

"She told me she was on her way. I hope she's all right!"

"Why shouldn't she be? And why should she be coming here?"

"She's had a car accident, but I gather she isn't injured, only shocked."

"Oh – Philip! But why is she coming here and what –?" she broke off and saw how tired he looked. "I'll get you a drink while you tell me."

"Thank you, Leonie. I could do with one! Hilda rang me at the office this morning and asked if I could see her. It was very urgent, she said, and she sounded distressed. When I said I was booked up all day, she wouldn't get off the line until I'd promised to see her somehow. She refused to come to my office after hours – she said some odd, wild thing about 'them' finding out! So, I suggested that she dine with me at a small, inconspicuous restaurant I know of."

"Did she say what she wanted to see you about?"

"No."

"But why are you expecting to meet her here?"

"A quarter of an hour ago she rang up the restaurant and seemed very distressed. I hadn't arrived but she gave the receptionist a message for me. She said she wasn't in any state to meet me in a public place, so would I come to your flat and she would tell me what had happened. She knew you were here because you had said this morning that you would be staying in town until after your TV show."

Philip paused to light a cigarette. Pouring out a Scotch for him, splashing in soda, Leonie thought: She's going to tell Philip what she told me – that she knows who killed Marcus. She told the truth when she said that: she lied this morning when she said it had been just her imagining –

She took the drink across the Philip. "You'll be better able to cope when you've had that!"

He thanked her and she asked:

"Where did the accident happen?"

"Somewhere in Hammersmith, I believe. I don't know anything much myself." He put out a hand and touched Leonie's arm. "I'm sorry you had to be involved – I suppose she's so utterly alone over here that she didn't know where else to go!"

"But Hilda didn't ring me," Leonie said. "It

would have been sensible to have found out first if I was here."

"I don't believe she was in any state to be sensible!" But he said it absently, and his eyes told her that he was far more aware of Leonie standing there, so near him, than of Hilda's visit. "It's good to see you again, Leonie, like this, I mean. Alone —"

She turned away towards the mirror, brushed lightly at her hair and said:

"We're going to be matter-of-fact, Philip. We've got to be."

He came and stood behind her and for a moment his eyes seemed to linger over every feature of her face reflected in the little round, gilded mirror. Then he put down his drink, turned her round to face him and said:

"I'm going to tell Claire about us."

Joy welled up: this was what she had dreamed he would say! And then her singing joy left her. She said very quietly:

"It isn't as easy as that, Philip."

"Tell me what isn't easy?"

She dragged herself away from him, averting her eyes from the demand in his, her heart thudding:

"Don't you see, we must wait until Claire has had this operation. Let her get that over — a spell in hospital isn't a happy thing to

114

have hanging over you!"

"And in the meantime?" his voice was rough, "I'm to pretend that everything is all right between us, is that it? I'm to let her go on believing that when she is free of Johnnie, I'll marry her!" He turned, picked up his drink and then set the glass down again. His eyes were angry.

"So I'm to play-act! Tell Claire pretty lies! 'Yes, darling, when you're better we'll go dancing and swimming together' . . . 'Hi, Mrs. Philip-Drew-to-be, what's this I hear about you wanting a yellow living-room? Or a violet bedroom? Or a black bathroom?' For God's sake, Leonie —"

Again the doorbell rang.

They stopped and looked at one another helplessly, their love dragging and tightening like a cord between them.

"I'm no saint," Philip said harshly. "But I'm no liar, either!"

"Oh Philip —" she cried and then tore herself away from his gaze and sped to open the door.

As Leonie pulled at it, Hilda nearly fell in. Distraught, dishevelled, she had come by taxi and her handbag was still hanging open as Leonie pulled her into the hall and shut the door. Hilda's hat was in her hand, a pretty thing of black straw and yellow daisies.

"I've just had an accident. Leonie, I might have been killed. Someone — wanted me to be killed —"

"You'd better go into the living-room. Philip is there." She had to help her in, Hilda's legs weren't carrying her properly.

"Come and sit down, Hilda," Philip took control, "and tell us what all this is about?"

"They gave you my message?" She looked at him dully, picking at her hat.

"That's why I'm here. What's this about an accident?"

"But it wasn't really an accident, Philip! It was deliberate. That's just it — that's what's so — awful —"

Leonie had gone to a cupboard and found a small bottle of brandy. She poured generously into a goblet.

"Suppose you tell us —" Philip began. "Start at the beginning. What were you coming to see me about?"

Hilda shot a swift, guarded look towards Leonie. Philip interpreted it.

"Leonie stays," he said. "Have a cigarette."

Hilda looked down at his open case and shook her head.

"I don't like smoking, much!"

"Never mind. Just this once, take one."

She obeyed and he lit it, watching her hand shake.

"I wanted to ask your advice about Julian and me," she said. "I wanted to know what I should do. I'm a stranger here. That's what's so awful – having no friends."

"No one need be friendless," Philip said. "But go on –"

His brusqueness was deliberate. Sympathy would just make Hilda crumple up. As it was, she drank some brandy, and then said:

"I daren't let Julian know I was coming to see you, that's why I was a bit late this evening in starting. They all seemed to be milling round, just because I wanted to slip away. In the end, I knew I'd be late if I took a bus and I daren't ring for a taxi. So I took Julian's car. He knows I usually go for a run in it in the evenings – he never needs it when he's working, anyway. And I came up to London in it. I thought there was something wrong as I was passing Barnes Common and then, when I reached Hammersmith, the steering just went and I shot into a lamp-post. It was awful! I thought I was going to die!" she shuddered, drew on her cigarette and choked a little.

"And then?" Philip urged.

"Someone got me out of the car and someone else phoned to a garage. People were awfully

kind and there was a policeman there and —
and I was crying and making a fool of myself."

"You were shocked. It was natural."

"The garage man said that a pin — or a nut
— I don't quite know *what* he said it was, had
worked loose. But the car was a comparatively
new one. It couldn't happen — not on its own!"

"You know the name of the garage?"

"They gave me a card. I've got it somewhere
in my bag. And when they took the car away,
the policeman wanted me to go to hospital to
see if I was really all right, but I wouldn't. I
wanted to get to you, Philip. I was so
frightened."

"Faults occur, even in new cars. You were
very unlucky to be driving; you were also lucky
to have escaped serious injury."

"That's just it." She sat up. Strength seemed
to come to her. "I was luckier than — than
someone — thought I'd be! I could have been
killed."

"But you weren't," the briskness returned to
Philip's voice. "One of the most useless things
in life is to imagine the awful things that might
have been. You shock yourself unnecessarily."

"But you don't understand." She turned her
head and her eyes became knowing. "*You* do,
don't you, Leonie? After our talk, *you* know
what I mean."

"If you'd tell Philip —"

"Tell me what?" he rapped out.

Hilda pretended not to hear. "I get so bored in the evenings, shut up in that house. Julian never sits with me and Venetia glues herself to television and carps and criticises through everything — though she won't listen if I say anything! It's so lonely and — creepy — you see —"

"And so," Philip brought her back to his point. "Julian knew you might take the car out?"

"Yes. I told you. I do most evenings. I go anywhere — just to get away from that house —" she shivered. "They don't want me, you know! Julian would love me to leave him; and Venetia wants that, too!"

"I refuse to believe," Philip said very matter-of-factly, "that anyone deliberately tampered with the car in order to frighten you away!"

"But someone did do just that —" Hilda sat forward, looking at Leonie, and her eyes were wide and even more terrified. "Perhaps that was it! Leonie, someone heard what we were saying last night. Someone heard — what *I* said and —"

"Tell Philip!" Leonie urged. "Or if you won't *I* will!"

"No!" Hilda shot to her feet. The glass shook

119

in her hand. "No, Leonie. You promised to keep what — what I told you a secret. Leonie — don't tell —"

"*Someone* had better tell me," Philip said, quietly.

"I said something stupid last night, something that — that wasn't true!" Hilda cried. "I was my imagination, my *stupid* imagination! It's *my* secret, Leonie! It's not for you to tell!"

"You're not making sense!" Philip rapped out. "First you suggest that someone overheard something you said to Leonie last night and hint that because of it, whoever it was tried to kill you to-day. Then you say that what you told Leonie last night wasn't true, which indicates that if anyone heard it wouldn't make them either frightened of you or vindictive because it wasn't true! Which do you want me to believe?"

She wept. "I'm muddled and frightened. Philip — don't badger me!"

"I think — " Leonie began. And then stopped because Philip shook his head at her. His look said plainly that Hilda was on the border of hysteria and there was no sense to be got out of her.

"First of all," he said, "we've got to face the fact that accidents can happen even to comparatively new cars. Secondly, the garage will probably be able to find out if it was a fault in the assembly of the car."

She looked up at him, quieter now.

"You *will* help me, won't you, Philip?"

"That all depends on how you want help. You must understand, Hilda, that I'm the Sarat lawyer. I can't act for you as well, that is if you are wanting legal advice in some action against them."

"So you're on their side!"

"It isn't a matter of 'sides'." He glanced across the room and saw Leonie look at her watch. "We'll talk this over, Hilda, quietly."

"I really wanted to see you to find out if there is any case I can bring against Julian – I mean so that if I leave him I won't be destitute. There are charges in the States – but England is more – stuffy about these things, isn't it? I mean – incompatibility – cruelty –"

"Look, Leonie wants to go. We'll find a place and have a meal together. Then perhaps Leonie, we can pick you up after your show and run you back to Richmond."

"Thank you, Philip."

She went into her bedroom, changed into the dress she was to wear on the screen that night and did her face.

Hilda was frightened, but Philip was there to

deal with her. It wasn't true, of course, that someone had tried to harm her. Julian, because he wanted to frighten her away? Or — someone else who had overheard what she had said last night. Someone listening . . . ?

She pulled herself together. Such things happened. But not to them — not in ordinary families. . . .

She put down her comb and looked at herself.

Philip loves me. . . . One day we'll be together. . . .

Or would they? It all sounded too easy, and experience had taught her that she wasn't the sort of person to whom things came easily. Words and wishes, promises — how glibly they came into the mind — and yet, in fact, they could be as far away as the moon. . . .

The church clock on the far side of the Square sounded the half-hour. Leonie flung her sapphire-coloured coat round her shoulders, seized her handbag and gloves and returned to the living-room.

Hilda was alone.

"Where's Philip?"

"He took the glasses into the kitchen. Leonie — I don't know what I've been saying — at least only vaguely. Please — don't tell Philip what I said to you — about Marcus. It wasn't true and I want to forget I ever said it!"

"I still think —" she began.

"As you're not coming back here to-night, Leonie, we couldn't leave debris about!" he grinned at her and set the glasses on a corner table. He had even cleaned out the ash trays.

"You're very well trained, Philip!"

"My mother used to say: 'You can have your friends in and enjoy yourselves in your own way. But don't leave me to clear up after you!' Once, when we all went on to some other party and left everything because we were in a hurry, Mother said nothing. But next time I had people in, there weren't any glasses to drink out of, nor any ash trays. You know where she had hidden them all? In the bottom of the grandfather clock in the hall."

Leonie laughed. Hilda tried to smile and couldn't quite make it.

In the car, Leonie said:

"Won't Claire wonder where you are?"

"Oh, she's down in Sussex working late again."

Hilda clutched his arm. "Don't go so fast!"

"Clean license," he laughed at her, "and never clutch at a driver's arm!"

"You're so lucky," Hilda said, "having a career and being beholden to no one. Oh, Leonie, you don't *know* how lucky you are! I was a model once in New York. You'd never think it to look at me now, would you?"

Philip said something kind to her in a low voice. Leonie, in the back of the car, let them talk. She sat, hugged in her big coat and wished that to-night's performance was over.

VII

When, two hours later, she came out of the studios, Philip and Hilda were waiting for her.

Hilda was no longer a bundle of twitching, jerky gestures. Philip had managed to calm her and it was only when they neared Richmond Hill that she said suddenly:

"Nobody must know that I came to London on purpose to see you, Philip!"

"They're bound to –"

"No they're not! They mustn't know – Philip, you won't tell them, will you? After all, my visit to you should be confidential, shouldn't it, as you're a lawyer?"

"But you can't just say you happened to meet him, by chance!" Leonie began.

"I know. But when we get home, you must let me explain."

Philip was occupied with manipulating the traffic streaming down the Hill. As they turned into the drive under the arch with the stone heron, they saw Claire's car parked under the trees.

"You'll come with me, won't you, Philip?" Hilda said quickly. "Don't just drive away."

There was no time to stay arguing. Philip had begun to speak, saying:

"I don't think I'll come in. It would be better —" when suddenly, in the headlamps, they saw Claire.

She was standing in the full glare and, like that, she looked unreal — like a small, dark ghost in a blaze of light.

So Philip couldn't just drive off. As they all got out of the car, Claire turned towards them.

"Hallo? Where did you all meet up?"

"In town," Philip said briefly. "Come along upstairs and I'll tell you about it."

Hilda dragged at Leonie's arm. "He mustn't! He mustn't!" she whispered."I'll do the telling in my own way!"

They went up the stairs together, Leonie dragging off her coat. On the middle landing she paused and dropped it on to a low carved Italian chest, and then followed up the remainder of the flight behind Claire.

She was limping as though every movement hurt her. And yet she worked hard and seldom complained. She had courage and endurance; she had pride. I'm trying to like her, Leonie thought, but I can't, I don't believe I ever did in the old days. It's not just because of Philip —

In the drawing-room, old Venetia sat in her favourite chair. The television had been turned off and Julian half sprawled on the settee.

They both looked up as the little group entered. Then Julian sprang to his feet.

"Good lord, my wandering wife is back! Where in the world —" he stopped suddenly and looked quickly from one to the other. "What's the matter?"

Philip spoke. "There's been an accident. Nobody has been hurt, but Hilda is shocked and your car, I'm afraid, is damaged."

"Of all the stupid, fumbling women —"

"Wait and hear what happened," Philip cut in. "Shall I tell him, Hilda?"

"No," she said, and there was a sudden, unexpected strength about her. "I will." She was sitting on the settee with Leonie. She wasn't shaking at all now, and she told her story quite calmly. She had gone for her usual evening run, but decided to go into town and drive around the West End, just to see the lights and people. The accident had happened at Hammersmith. She was shocked and didn't feel like making the journey home. She most certainly wasn't going to hospital, either. "And then I remembered that Leonie was in town that evening. I looked up her address in the telephone directory and I took a taxi to her flat.

I knew she'd let me just sit and rest a bit. I hoped she'd be there. She was." Hilda lowered her eyes. "I was awfully lucky to find her in! And — Philip was there, too!"

Leonie felt Claire's eyes flash to her. Philip tried to cut in, saying: "The point was —" but Hilda rushed on, her voice rising, talking over his, repeating herself, words tumbling over each other. But not, Leonie knew, because she was still hysterical, but because she had planned what she would say to clear herself and she was daring Philip to deny her story.

"And Philip was there, too . . ." Didn't she see she was implicating others in her desire to safeguard herself?

When there was a moment's silence, Leonie thought, she would tell those three people — Venetia and Julian and Claire — the truth. She would say, "Oh, but Hilda asked Philip to meet her at my flat!" But the damage was done. She could protest, Philip could protest — and everyone would believe that they were merely trying to cover up a secret meeting Hilda had broken in upon. Better say nothing and leave Philip to explain to Claire.

She was aware that Julian was saying:
"I thought this afternoon that the steering of the car was a bit odd."

Hilda turned on him. "And you didn't tell me!"

"For heaven's sake, I didn't have a chance! I've been working like blazes! Why didn't you come and tell me you were taking the car out? You usually do. And I'd have stopped you using it until I'd had a chance to run it to a garage for a check."

"Would you? Would you *really?*" Hilda cried in wild disbelief. "Or were you hoping —" she went on, and then covered her mouth with her hand like a child, stopping unwise words.

"Hoping what?" Venetia snapped.

"Perhaps I might make a suggestion." Philip spoke. "Julian, suppose you ring the garage and find out what really went wrong. Hilda doesn't seem to know the difference between a pin and a nut and a screw?" He spoke lightly, quite kindly.

"Of course," Julian rose, took the printed card with the garage address and telephone number on it and went out of the room.

The small silence which followed his departure was too much for Hilda.

"I might have been killed," she burst out. "Doesn't anyone realise that? I might have crashed into another car —"

"But you weren't. And you didn't," Venetia said shortly.

"Hilda has been very shocked," Philip said quickly. "That's why she called —"

"— why I called at Leonie's," she almost shouted. Her eyes, staring at him, pleaded openly. *Don't tell . . . don't tell that I had a date with you. . . .*

"Well, it's all over." Venetia sat back in her chair, put her lovely snowy head against a cushion and closed her eyes. "Don't let's drag out the melodrama!"

"Why shouldn't I be frightened because I was nearly killed?" Hilda defended. "Why *shouldn't* I care? After all, I'm the only one who loves me!"

The pathetic words hung on the air. Leonie watched Philip light a cigarette with steady hands. It was obvious that he was going to humour Hilda and had no longer any intention of explaining why he had been in Leonie's flat. Afterwards, he would probably tell Claire in private — and be quite certain that she would believe him.

Julian returned, saying:

"There's a definite fault in the steering and the car is to be sent back to the works."

"So that's all over!" Venetia sighed.

Two people in the room moved. Philip rose and said he must be going. Claire moved to his side.

"I'll see you off, darling."

She had to pass Leonie and she turned and

glanced down at her. There was a faint smile on her face that seemed to say: I'm not distressed about what Hilda said. I know Philip loves me!

Hilda also rose and fled, muttering a general good night.

"Julian," Venetia ordered. "Go after her and get her to bed. Give her a sleeping pill from that box in my medicine cupboard. You see?" she turned to Leonie when they were alone in the room, "the sort of life Julian has with a woman like that! Weak and whining and full of fears —"

"She's still very shocked, you know, Grandmother. She could have been killed."

"Yes," Venetia said slowly, without horror, "she could have been, couldn't she?" and her paper-thin lids closed over her eyes.

In that moment she looked incredibly old; withdrawn from the world of youth and vitality; full of secrets. . . .

Leonie wanted to go to bed, but someone always stayed with Venetia until she chose to go. It was like a courtesy to the old that you never left her entirely alone in the evenings. And to-night Venetia just sat there, making no move; curiously alienated by her hidden thoughts, and old — suddenly very, very old. . . .

Leonie asked, purely in order to break the long, awkward silence:

"Where's Fran?"

"She said she was going out to see some friends. I don't know who they were: she was very evasive about them! And by the way, Leonie, since we are on the subject of Fran, has she always been on such warm terms with the gardener's children?"

"Why, yes. I remember she used to play with them a lot in the old days."

"They were shrieking and racing about again late this morning!" Venetia complained. "I can't imagine what Marcus was thinking of, having a gardener with children!"

"Jim is one of the finest he could possibly get, and Marcus was a perfectionist. His wife, Meg, was alive when he first came here," Leonie defended. "Jim was with him for ten years — until — he — was killed."

"Ten years in one place! Then perhaps it's time we had a change."

"Don't you like him, Grandmother?"

"*Like* him?" the old eyes widened. "Oh, I suppose so. Personal likes aren't important in one's staff," she added imperiously. "I'm only concerned with their standard of work."

"I don't think you'd improve on Jim."

"Maybe not, but this is *not* the place for

children!" Venetia tapped a foot impatiently. "Nor do I wish Fran to be a playmate for my employee's offspring!"

"Fran is used to young people —"

"She's twenty-five and I don't expect to see her lying on a newly-cut lawn with straws in her hair, like mad Ophelia!"

Leonie's sudden spurt of laughter died as she saw that old Venetia was not just being amusing. She turned away as her grandmother leant her head back and closed her eyes.

The axe had been lifted, it remained now only for the blow to fall. Jim's days here were numbered! Well, he'd be able to work full-time at Kew. But he would lose his cottage and that had been a beloved home to him and to Gay and Chris. . . . And if a cottage did not go with his job, what would happen to the children? Without a wife to look after them, he had to be somewhere near them. Or marry again, and Leonie was quite certain that a man like Jim Farraday did not go through life without stirring up love in many of the women he met!

There was a sound outside and Claire entered.

"It's beginning to rain," she observed in her soft, flat voice.

Venetia opened her eyes: vitality flowed back into her.

"Spring rain!" her gaze went to the window. "Close it, Claire, will you?"

She watched Claire cross the room, her eyes narrow, conjecturing. The slender arms were raised to catch at the side cords; the window slipped up smoothly.

"When do you and Philip plan to get married?" Venetia asked.

Claire turned at the window and smiled.

"If all goes well, next winter."

"Not the best time of the year!"

"No, but there are such difficulties! If there weren't we'd be married to-morrow." She was answering her grandmother but her eyes rested on Leonie.

"Quite! Quite!" Venetia said quickly. "And where will the wedding take place?"

Claire came back into the room and perched on the wide arm of the chair.

"I've got cousins up in Norfolk. I could get married from their house."

"Or from here?"

Claire's eyes lit up in her strange, pale face.

"Here? But how lovely! Could I? Could I *really?*"

"My child, your grandfather was a very close friend. It's the least I can do! It'll have to be a registry office wedding, of course, but the house is large enough for you to have quite a big reception if that's what you would like."

"Oh I would! You see, I shall be able to walk properly then and I just long for lots of glamour. I didn't have it with Johnnie. He just wanted to slip away and tell no one until it was over. But then I saw, when it was too late, he was scared of opposition because I was the one with money. That's what he married me for, Mrs. Sarat, and it takes a girl a long time to get over that realisation! This time, though, it's love!"

"Well, then, you shall have as much glamour as we can manage for you. We could open the music-room and have the reception there." Venetia nodded her head as though agreeing with herself. "People have short memories — they will have forgotten to be squeamish by that time!"

"But there's lots of space without using the music-room," Claire said a little too quickly. "Really, Mrs. Sarat, I wouldn't — I mean, I don't —" she broke off with an agitation uncharacteristic of her. "There's the hall, for instance; it's huge and in winter it can look so lovely! If we could have all that beautiful special lighting Marcus used to bring out on special occasions."

Old Venetia sat up straight in her chair.

"How do you know about those lights? I've

only come across them recently up in the attic. I don't even know when he used them, so how do you —?"

Colour rushed to Claire's cheeks.

"Oh I heard about them — from my grandfather, I think —"

"They're much too modern for his time!"

"Then — someone must have told me," she smiled. "Of course, that's it! I remember, it was someone I knew who used to be asked to Marcus's private concerts. She — she said that the lighting was really lovely — all glamorous and stagey —"

"Indeed?"

"Anyway, it will be wonderful to be married from here. Thank you so very much, Mrs. Sarat." Claire rose. "Would you mind if I went to bed now? I've had a very busy day."

Old Venetia's eyes watched every step across the room, her eyes focusing almost cruelly on Claire's distorted walk. When she had disappeared, she said softly, as though to herself:

"Claire has been here before!"

Leonie sat very still.

Old eyes slewed round at her. "Did you know that, Leonie? She pretends she never knew Marcus, but she did!"

"You mean — because she knew about

those special lights?"

"And other things," the white head nodded slowly. "From the moment she came, she walked about this house as though she were familiar with it. It never dawned on her to pretend she didn't know it — I suppose she thought I was too old to notice and the rest of you were too busy. I tested her yesterday, when no one was around to tell her. I asked her to fetch me a folding chair — it was warm enough to sit on the terrace. Claire went straight up to the attic — she knew, you see, that Marcus stored them there and not in the garden shed. But *I* only saw them a few days ago when Boadicea and I went up there to look round and see what junk Diana had left in the house. They were hidden behind an old screen — but Claire knew where to find them!"

"But if Claire has been here before, why doesn't she say so?"

"That's what interests me, too! She was so excited at the thought of having her wedding from here that she forgot to be cautious! Why does she have to be?" Venetia rose stiffly. She looked across the room into space and her frail body was rigid, as though it had been turned to stone.

"Claire," her voice was a whisper. "Of course, it could have been — Claire —"

"What could have been?"

For a moment Venetia did not hear her. Leonie repeated her question. The white head turned slowly, the eyes seemed to come back from some image in the past and focus with difficulty.

"I'm tired," she said without answering Leonie's question. "I am going to bed."

It could have been Claire! What could? What had suddenly struck across that ancient and worldly old mind with such force that for a moment she had lost contact with the present?

Leonie went slowly downstairs to turn off the lights. The front door was open and she pushed it wider and went out into the night.

Her mind went back to what Hilda had said. Did she really suspect Julian of trying to harm her? Or had that been a kind of hysterical outburst which, when she thought about it more, she hadn't believed? Then, had she clung to it as a cover-up for something she was too frightened to admit? Something to do with what she had said to Leonie over a cup of tea in the kitchen at Heron House at midnight. . . . *I know who killed Marcus.* . . . The statement she was retracting so violently, so desperately . . . in case someone had heard. . . .

The rain falling was scarcely more than a mist. It was very still out here in the garden, not even a leaf stirred and back in the house the only light on this side was the one she had left on over the landing and the one from the hall.

She walked a little way down the drive, her feet crunching softly on the damp gravel. The light rain touched her face so gently. Then she turned to go back to the house.

The door stood wide open and from where she was, she could see the edge of the refectory table and the clean, beautiful lines of the staircase. That was all! Something puzzled her and she stood still, trying to take hold of it. Something that had been said ... something Claire had said.

And then she remembered. Claire had told her that when she had been waiting in the car on that Saturday afternoon a long time ago, when Philip had called at the house and she had seen Marcus from a distance, she had admired the carpets on the walls, the silken Shiraz and Isfahan and the great bowl of flowers on the table. *But, from the drive you could see none of these things!*

So proof again that Claire had been here before! Then why not say: "Yes, I knew Marcus." Why lie about it – unless there was something she was afraid of? Could she have been here on the day of Marcus's death? It occurred to Leonie that she could write to Florrie up in Thurso and find out. And then she remembered that Florrie had been enjoying her evening off when Marcus was killed. But I could ask her, Leonie thought, if Claire used to come to the house after I left. And yet to have done so would be like spying and she knew she couldn't do it. Leave it, she thought. It doesn't matter, it isn't important anyway. Or wasn't it? Words used during the inquiry into the murder came back to her. *A woman could have done it. A woman could have thrown that little stone statuette which killed Marcus Sarat.* . . .

This was wild imagining; the product of an overstimulated mind. Leonie pulled herself together. People like Claire didn't kill. . . .

"You should be in bed and asleep!"

Leonie started and saw Julian coming along the black cavern of a path from the studio.

"I wanted a breath of air first."

"And a drop of rain," he reached out and touched her. "Your hair's quite wet."

"It's only a light mist. Did you see Hilda to bed?"

"No, of course I didn't! She's old enough to put herself there! I went to tidy up my studio. Anyway, she's better without seeing me — she obviously thinks it was my fault she had the accident."

"Poor Hilda! It was a horrible experience."

"It was," he agreed. "But I've a feeling if it had happened to you, you would have behaved differently. You're such a sane person, Leonie. I'm glad you're staying here, I hope you never leave. Venetia hopes that, too!"

He put out his hands and drew Leonie towards him.

"Let's meet sometimes in London. Have dinner with me — or lunch —"

"We meet here —"

"With people watching us?"

"Well, what's wrong with that?"

His voice changed;

"You were only too willing to meet Philip in town, weren't you — in fact, to let him come to your flat."

She snatched her hands away and tried to pass him, but he seized her wrist.

"You're playing with fire there, Leonie, and I believe you know it. Claire will never let Philip go and if he ever tried, then God help him! Whereas I — you know don't you that when — well, when Venetia dies, I shall be rich? That's all Hilda is waiting for. When I'm free of her —"

"Stop talking to me like this and let me go! Julian! *Let* — *me* — *go* —"

But he dragged her to him and was trying to kiss her.

"Listen to me, please, Leonie. It isn't just my idea that one day you and I will be together. It's Venetia's, too! She knows we are two of a kind, that the theatre is in our blood."

"I said: "Let me go!""

For an answer his head came down with a swift movement and his lips pressed hers with a startling violence of movement, as though behind his charming weakness was an undreamed-of strength.

She fought him angrily. He freed her lips, but his arms pinioned her.

"When you walked into the living-room on that first evening, it was as though everything fell into place. This was what I should have waited for! But how can one ever know the possibilities that lie ahead?"

She turned wildly in his arms and at that moment something small and white streaked into the bushes in front of them. Hilda's little cat.

Julian dropped his arms as though they had been shot down. There was a movement as someone in the shadows swooped to pick the cat up.

Someone walking in the garden in the rain . . . Hilda? Hilda who always came out at night to watch her little cat and see that he didn't stray on to Richmond Hill?

VIII

It was as though wings took Leonie to the house. She fled up to her room and stood for a while in the darkness, pulling herself together.

She was pretty certain that whoever had been walking in the garden had seen them, and that it was Hilda. All she hoped was that Julian would tell the truth and not involve her . . . she had had quite enough of that already to-night!

She heard footsteps come up the stairs and branch off down the corridor; heard someone close a window.

Leonie flung herself on her bed, hiding her face in the silk coverlet. She lay like that, enmeshed in a cocoon of silk and linen, faintly scented with sandalwood, and heard Fran come quietly past her room. Fran's door closed and then there was silence. She thought she must have dropped off to sleep, lightly like a cat, as though in that superficial unconsciousness every nerve was alert for sound, like an animal's jungle awareness. Suddenly a sound did disturb her light sleep. She moved, opening her eyes, and listened.

Softly but insidiously came the sound of sobbing. Fran was crying her heart out in the next room.

Leonie swung her legs off the bed and sat wondering whether to go in to her. Would *I* welcome someone opening *my* door and asking what was the matter? The answer was a reluctant "No." Would *I* want someone intruding on my unhappiness? Answer again: "No." And yet Fran was different. She would probably welcome a shoulder to weep on. She hadn't had to face life alone, to learn to guard her real feelings from a brilliant but cynical guardian; to be careful lest a look, a flicker of an eyelid betrayed a feeling she fought to keep to herself lest it be mocked. Fran was warm and gentle; she had had loving parents, an easy home life, and in her work, no feeling of competition, no fear of where the next week's rent was coming from. All that added up to the fact that she was probably used to confiding, to wanting to tell someone what troubled her.

Leonie went to the window, opening it cautiously and listening. The sobs came more intermittently from the next room; little weary, drained sounds as though the accumulators of energy within her were now exhausted and the strength to cry was gone.

When Leonie knocked on Fran's door, there were swift muffled sounds inside and then a lightly-called: "Come in."

Fran was at the dressing-table doing something to her hair.

"Oh, hallo —" She kept her face rigidly towards the oval mirror, gave a good imitation of a yawn and said:

"Good heavens, I'm tired!"

Leonie walked across the room. She stood at the mahogany tallboy, picked up a white china horse and said:

"I heard you, Fran. I thought perhaps I could help —"

"Help?" The pretty, exhausted face puckered in an elaborate pretence. "What on earth do I want help for?"

With the little white horse still in her hand, Leonie met her gaze in the mirror.

Suddenly Fran swung round.

"You heard me crying?"

"Yes."

Fran gave in. "All right I was!" her tone was on the defensive. "But you can't help, thanks!"

"I suppose not —"

"I cry easily, you should have remembered that!"

But she didn't; she was merely wanting to minimise her distress.

"I'm sorry, Fran," Leonie said gently. "I should have minded my own business. You'd have come to me if you'd wanted me to know what was the matter." She set down the ornament and walked to the door. "I'd better go to bed."

Fran didn't answer. She watched Leonie's reflection. Then, as the handle of the door turned, she flung round.

"Just a minute."

Leonie's chestnut hair fell like a wing across her cheek as she stood waiting, looking down at her green suède shoe, careful not to come rushing back into the room as though avid to know what it was all about, and so send Fran back into her proud, unhappy shell.

"Do you think," Fran asked suddenly, "that Grandmother will get rid of Jim?"

It was almost as though she had been present to-night, in the great living-room, listening to old Venetia's conversation.

"I don't know. Why do you ask?"

"She said something this morning, something about wanting a gardener-chauffeur, preferably an unmarried one."

"Well, if she does, Jim can always work full-time at Kew Gardens."

"But he loves his cottage!" Fran cried. "It's the only home the children have known!"

It was queer, Leonie thought, that in those two adjoining rooms they must have had the same thoughts – Leonie to puzzle over it, Fran to weep. . . .

Thoughts about Jim Farraday! As though he had suddenly become very important in the house – not just a gardener, living his own life with his own small family, but drawn into the orbit of the Sarats and assuming proportions that made him dominate the thoughts of three people in one evening – Old Venetia and Fran and herself. . . .

Fran was watching her, waiting for her to say something.

"It would be hard for a time, but he'd never be out of work. He's too good at his job for that."

"But the children! You know how Florrie used to keep an eye on them. Boadicea does the same, though Grandmother doesn't know it! Boadicea may be simple in lots of ways, but she has a native wisdom – she knows almost by instinct that she'd be harangued if it were known she slips down every day to the cottage. So, she just 'Says nuffin'.'" Fran's fingers moved over the dressing-table, touching things, shifting them, brushing a few specks of powder away, restless, absorbed. "Leonie, she *mustn't* sack Jim!"

"Jim must have been prepared for something like this to happen!" Leonie said gently. "When a new owner takes over, it often means new staff."

"Then you really think that Jim might have to go?"

"I don't know. I'm just trying to see the possibility and thinking that he must see it, too! He's an intelligent man —"

"I wish she'd never come here! I hate her! Leonie, I *hate* her!" Fran's eyes blazed: her rare anger had burst from her like a flame. "Why couldn't she stay where she was in New Orleans? Why come here and upset us all!"

"Be reasonable, Fran! She doesn't realise that anything she might do would affect one of us!"

"She wouldn't care, anyway!" Fran cried.

Leonie met the furious light in the usually laughing eyes. "You're making a rather hasty judgment, aren't you? You've only been in the house a few days, you can't hate Grandmother. After all, be fair, it's her house and Jim is a completely new person to her — she can't be expected to keep him on out of sentiment or appreciation of long service. If she wants a chauffeur-gardener —"

"All she wants is to get rid of the sound of the children!" Fran cried. "She's not human!"

"You must remember, she's old. She

probably likes peace around her."

"Peace? Not she! She likes war — she's had it all her life! Father told me there was always trouble with someone about something when she was on the stage here. She thrived on it. And now Jim has to suffer!"

"My dear Fran, it's three years since his wife died. He's very good-looking; he's a nice man, he will marry again!"

"But he won't," Fran cried. "That's just it, Leonie. *He won't!*" Fran's hands flew to her face, but not quickly enough to hide the naked, despairing pain there.

"Fran —"

She sank on to the bed, leaning against the carved wooden post.

Leonie's arms were round her. The distraught face was hidden and Fran wasn't crying. She was trembling with some secret misery. But it wasn't secret. Leonie knew!

A small gilt clock ticked the seconds away. Outside the room, the house was very quiet. Sleeping — or watching — or listening?

Through her hands, Fran said:

"Don't tell! Leonie, don't tell anyone!"

"Don't tell — about —?" she waited.

Fran's brown hair curled against the young neck; her shoulders quivered in a small, reflex action. Her face, as she turned towards

Leonie, was impassive. She said:

"Jim won't marry me!"

Although she had guessed, the words came almost as a shock to Leonie.

"You're in love with him — and I never knew!"

The hazel eyes widened.

"You mean Marcus never told you?"

"Good heavens, no! But Fran, you mean you were in love with Jim then — in those days —?"

"Why do you think I went away? Why do you think all — all that business over Marcus was such — such hell for me? Of course Marcus knew! He knew everything that went on! He just sat there in that beautiful, horrible, almost sound-proof room of his and shook with amusement. He said — he said:

" 'So you want to make yourself a laughing-stock with everyone! The rich girl and the gardener! It's a sort of Victorian novelette pattern.' He said: 'You fool! Don't you see what Jim loves? And it *isn't* you!' I hated him from that moment. I hated him so much!"

"And now you're home again," Leonie prodded gently, "does Jim still love you?"

Fran closed her eyes.

"A year ago he said he did. I tried to make him see how out-of-date his principles were. I said he was being an inverted snob about it! He just said: 'Fine, so I am! But I'm not marrying a girl with a rich father.' We argued and I nearly made him see sense – through the children because they liked me. And that was when Marcus found out. He ruined it all. Nobody heard my row with him because Florrie had her evening off."

"And Jim knew about your quarrel?"

Fran nodded. "After he had tackled me, Marcus sent for Jim. I stayed around because I was terrified that Jim would fall into the trap of Marcus's lofty, cynical manner. He did. Jim just let fly; I couldn't bear to hear them, so I ran away, back to the hostel. Oh Leonie, when two men hate each other so, when one is proud and violently angry and the other is like a quiet, stalking tiger –" she broke off, her face strained and drawn with the memory.

"When was this quarrel?"

Something seemed to jolt inside Fran as though she suddenly realised that she was saying too much. A mask came down over her face.

"Some time last year. I mean –" she suddenly swung round. "If you think Jim killed Marcus in a fit of fury then you're mistaken! He never did! *He didn't.*"

"All right! All right! The police questioned Jim and were satisfied he had nothing to do with the murder. He had an alibi."

"Yes. He had!" The mask was still there over Fran's young face.

Leonie heard herself say, without having seemed to think at the thought first:

"That man who gave evidence that Jim was in one of the glass-houses at Kew — he was a friend, wasn't he?"

"What has that got to do with it?" Fran leapt to his defence. "He *saw* Jim — that was good enough for the police. And for me!" She swung round on her, but there was fear rather than anger in her voice. "It's all *over!* Marcus is dead and the past is buried. Why did you have to stir up the ghosts, Leonie? *Why?* Nobody else wants to probe and question. Only you! And you remember what Grandmother said. 'What's done is done!' I told you about Jim and me because I — I trusted you — not so that you should start wondering if — if — Jim killed Marcus." She sat on the edge of the bed, her fingers locked tightly together, her eyes no longer softly hazel, but dark, as though pain had over-painted them.

Leonie rose and walked across the room and back. She said, very quietly:

"I'm sorry, Fran. I just asked you when it was that Marcus found out about you and Jim. I didn't mean to upset you. I was thoughtless.

Perhaps we'd both better get to bed."

"Leonie, Jim is innocent! However you work things out in your own mind, you'll never be able to prove that he — he murdered Marcus! Not even accidentally, in anger! But don't go trying to resurrect it all, please don't. Marcus is dead!"

For a moment their eyes met across the space of the room, and then Leonie said gently:

"Look, we're both getting over-tense about this. What we need is sleep."

"And you'll tell no one about Jim and me?"

"Of course not! But you'll have to be prepared for Grandmother to find out."

"If she does, I'll deal with it! She has no hold over me. I can leave here and go and see Jim and the children as often as I like. I know what you're thinking," she added suddenly. "You believe that if Grandmother knows that Jim and I were in love in the old days, she'll put two and two together in that sharp old brain of hers and start wondering if Jim killed Marcus. Well, let her! Nobody knows about that quarrel except you and I, and neither of us believes that Jim killed him." She watched Leonie. *Do* we?"

"Of course not." Leonie moved to Fran's side, put an arm lightly round her and said insistently, "Go to bed, honey, and sleep. And if you love Jim, stick to him so hard that you'll wear his pride down! And mind I'm asked to the wedding!"

Back in her own room, Leonie could not sleep. She had asked Fran one question. The man who had given evidence that he had seen Jim in the glass-house at Kew had been a colleague, hadn't he? There were people who would lie and cheat to save a friend. . . . But that would be perjury! Well, it had happened before in Court . . . ! Suppose Jim hadn't been at Kew that night. Suppose he had been here at Heron House, with no alibi. Suppose this man, this friend, believed, in spite of opportunity and motive, that Jim was innocent! Then, in the name of a blind, faithful friendship, he might commit perjury.

Fran had protested too much! *Jim didn't kill Marcus! We don't believe he did, do we? Do we?*

When Hilda met Leonie the following morning, she gave no sign of having seen Leonie and Julian the previous night. But she was obviously avoiding her, darting busily into rooms as Leonie came by, averting her eyes, too occupied with nebulous tasks to stay and talk.

It could, Leonie thought, be her own sense of guilt that noticed these things. Perhaps Hilda was always like that, fussy and still ill-at-ease among strangers in the house. At any rate, there was nothing she could do or say that would not make the situation worse, and she was again glad that she had rehearsals to keep her away from the house all day.

At the end of the week, Leonie called at her flat before going to the theatre. She picked up two letters from the hall table and took them upstairs with her.

In the living-room she paused to light a cigarette and slit the first envelope. It contained a welcome cheque. The second letter held half a sheet of paper and on it were letters cut out of a newspaper and pasted to form a message:

"If you value your career you will leave Heron House. Otherwise there will be a whispering campaign against you. *Did* you find Marcus dead? Or −?

There was a P.T.O. in the corner of the sheet, but for the life of her Leonie couldn't turn the note over.

"Did you find Marcus dead?" The horror of the question beat about her for a few minutes before it flashed across her almost hysterically that some friend's offspring was playing a macabre and not very childish joke. Nobody would *really* want to harm her in this way — it was just someone's evil idea of a joke. . . .

And then she turned the sheet of paper over as the three printed letters in the corner told her to.

IX

On the other side was just one short sentence.

"This is not a joke."

The whole horrible thing was roughly done, with some letters cut out separately to make the word, and one or two words cut out wholly from whatever newspaper had been used, as though the sender were in a hurry. Yet she had a feeling that there was nothing naïve about it, that it had been carefully and calculatingly done. The postmark on the envelope was "London."

Who hates me so much? she thought shakenly. Who is so afraid of me?

She managed to steady herself sufficiently to get to the telephone and dial Philip's office number.

"It's Leonie here. If you're free lunch-time, can I see you? It's urgent, Philip!"

He responded to her agitation with quick alarm.

"What's happened? Is it something at the house?"

"No. I'm ringing from my flat. I had an anonymous letter — a rather horrible one."

"Come round straight away!"

"I can't; I've got a rehearsal now. But I'll be free about half past twelve. I'll have an hour or so then."

"I'm taking Claire to lunch — she called me about half an hour ago. But come round as soon as you can after twelve-thirty and we'll have a little while in which to talk. And Leonie — don't mention this letter to anyone."

"I won't. And thank you, Philip."

And now, somehow, I've got to get through the morning's rehearsals . . . pretend all is right with my world? Those in the theatre would look at her and think: Leonie Sarat? What has she got to worry her? Good looks; health; no responsibilities and on her way to the top! In her sapphire coat slung over a cream dress, wide gold bangles at her wrists and with her bright hair, who'd give her one second of pity? Come to that, who gave anyone a compassionate thought as they passed in the street? Masks and faces . . . and the masks of some were beautiful and gay and no passing stranger dreamed of what lay behind.

A whispering campaign against her. . . .

Innocent people had been hounded to despair by such things. Well, she wouldn't be! She had worked hard for her place in the theatre, she wasn't going to lose it all. She would do what the letter told her and leave Heron House.

But who had sent it?

One name, one person stood out from the rest. Hilda! It *must* have been Hilda walking in the garden with her white cat. Hilda seeing in the blurred half moonlit darkness, her husband and Leonie; too far to hear what they were saying, too shocked and prejudiced to see that Leonie was resisting. Blaming "the girl in the case"; goaded by Venetia's contempt and Julian's disinterest, Hilda had done this horrible thing.

What did she mean by asking: *Did* you find Marcus dead? What did she know – or think she knew? Memory of Hilda's scared outburst: "I know who killed Marcus!" and then: "You know something you don't realise that you do. You are in danger, too!" But that implied that Hilda thought her innocent, not guilty and dangerous as the letter suggested.

The thought occurred to Leonie that perhaps such little knowledge as Hilda possessed was that which might incriminate one of two people – someone else or herself. Hilda had not believed ill of Leonie and had chosen the

159

other as suspect. But now jealousy had changed all that. Suspicion had switched to her. . . . If Venetia were right and Hilda was a neurotic and a hysteric, heaven knew what dangerous twists and turns her mind might take!

The striking of the church clock at the end of the Square startled her out of her bemused state. She stirred and then jumped a little as the telephone bell rang.

For a moment or two her feet wouldn't move. It was as though suddenly everything menaced – the doorbell; the telephone; the post; and she was afraid of them all.

When, at the third ring, she lifted the receiver, she heard Fran's voice.

"Oh, Leonie, I thought I remembered you saying you'd be going to your flat before the theatre, and I hoped I could catch you. I'm coming to town to-day. Could we lunch?"

"I'm sorry, Fran, but I can't."

There was a pause. Then: "Oh never mind, but I thought you said this morning that you'd probably have an hour for lunch and you'd try that new place off Piccadilly Circus."

"I did, but now I've got myself booked up."

Leonie understood the pause at the other end of the line. Fran was waiting for her to say with whom she was lunching, to mention a name casually, friendlily, as she always used to do in the past. But that was impossible. Instead, she said vaguely.

"Perhaps to-morrow?"

"No. Never mind!" Fran's voice sounded strained, then: "Leonie, is anything the matter?"

Leonie's heart leapt with sudden caution. "Why should you ask such a thing?"

"Oh, I don't know. Just a kind of feeling I had; a kind of hunch! *Is* everything all right, Leonie?"

"Of course! I just called in here for a few minutes to see if there was any mail and I was just off to the theatre when you rang."

"I see – then I won't keep you. Oh well! Good-bye."

The line went dead. Leonie replaced the receiver and stood staring at it as though it could answer her question. *Had* Fran merely telephoned to suggest that lunch? They used often to meet together at midday; but that was when they lived their separate lives, both tied up with their work so that they had no chance to meet at any other time. It was different now, they slept under the same roof and they had plenty of opportunity to talk together. "Is anything the matter?" Fran had asked. "*Is* everything all right?" But Leonie was quite certain that her voice had been perfectly controlled so that unless Fran had been extraordinarily sensitive, she could not have known that there was something very wrong indeed.

Leonie went to the mirror and stared at her reflection. She fought back the small snake of suspicion that Fran had had anything to do with that letter and that she had telephoned because she couldn't wait to find out what Leonie's reaction was! Not Fran . . . ! Or did one ever know the deep, dark, subterranean emotions that tore at those one thought one knew best?

And, haunted alike by friends and strangers, Leonie fled from her flat and found peace again only when she reached the theatre.

When she was on her way to see Philip at half past twelve she found that her mind could return freshly to that ghoulish note, freed from the intial shock of receiving it.

Her first reaction had been to obey and leave Heron House. Now, she faced the fact that if she did it would solve exactly nothing. Wherever she was, the evil would be there, unprobed, stalking secretly, watching. . . .

If she stayed at Richmond, then she might force the hand of whoever feared her so much as to threaten her. If it were Hilda who had sent the letter, then she wouldn't be able to hold her ugly secret for long.

If it were Fran — but it couldn't be! They had been so close in the past, they were still friends, and she knew her well enough to be certain that Fran had no ugliness, no malevolence in her mind. Yet how could she say how Fran or anyone, even herself, would behave if they were frightened for themselves or for someone they loved?

Whoever had sent the letter, he or she would carry out the threat and start a whispering campaign against her. Well, why let it matter if they did? There was nothing anyone could say that could harm her. Let them whisper; let them hint! *Did* she find Marcus dead when she arrived? *Did* she? When she saw people looking at her with a new curiosity, when she managed to drag from someone outside the family the face that people had begun to rake up the old mystery and ask questions about her, then would be the time to call the police. They were adept at tracing grape-vine communications to their source!

She found as she walked along the corridor to Philip's office, that she was shaking again. The door was open; she saw the sunlight filtering through the sparse trees, saw the glow of mahogany and turned to smile and thank

Philip's secretary as she stood by the door. Then she looked at Philip.

He was standing in the middle of the room and as she went towards him, sunbeams from the tall window danced on her face.

She took the letter out of her bag and laid it on his desk. Then she crumpled:

"Oh Philip! Why does someone hate me so much?"

In a single movement he had his arms round her, holding her close. His cheek against her hair soothed her, his arm was like a steel band encircling her, holding her safe against the world. Then, gently, he put her into a chair, gave her a cigarette and read the letter. She saw how carefully he handled it and she wanted to cry out to him: "Don't be so careful with it! There won't be fingerprints." But she held on to her self-control and just sat watching him.

Laying the letter down on his desk, he said.

"Of course you must go to the police."

"I'm not going to do that."

A trace of surprised impatience showed on his face.

"You wouldn't have come to me if you hadn't realised that this is serious. It is! You must take my advice, Leonie."

"Someone is afraid of me, Philip; afraid I know something about — Marcus's death.

That's it, isn't it?"

"Very possibly."

"But it could have been sent for some other reason." She was thinking of Hilda.

"Give me one, Leonie."

"In the theatre, you mean?"

She shook her head. "I don't know. I'm guessing. What I mean is, if it's someone who's just jealous, then it's not very serious. I mean, not as serious as if the note had been sent by someone — by whoever — killed — Marcus."

"I think we have to assume the worst, and go to the police."

"When I rang you up, Philip, I was terribly shocked. But on the way here from the theatre, I've been thinking more rationally about it. If I stay at Heron House, if I ignore the letter, then I shall perhaps force the hand of whoever wrote it. *That's* when the police should be called in. Then, not through this letter, but through the whispering gossip about me, they would trace who killed Marcus!"

"And that's the most important thing! Get justice done!" Rare anger flared up in him. "Well, and what prods you into being so noble, Leonie? What justice did you get from Marcus — *in the end?* And why risk your peace of mind by inviting this whispering campaign?"

"I know. I've been thinking it all out while I

was on my way here. I don't believe whoever sent that warning is completely ingenuous — the clues haven't been handed on a platter to the police, Philip! The typewriter could be anywhere in London; the envelope is ordinary; the letters used for the message are newsprint; only half a sheet of paper is used so it's my guess the watermark won't be on this half! And the fingerprints will be the postman's!"

"So you think this," he tapped the note on his desk, watching her, "won't help the police! Is that the only reason you're holding back?"

She shook her head. "I can't expect you to understand," she said gravely. "I think only people who have lost someone close to them in mysterious circumstances can ever understand the desperate need to *know*, to discover just what happened. Philip —" she cried "don't look at me like that! I know how you feel about Marcus, but his house was my home, he brought me up. Whatever he was, he was also the person closest to me; the only one to whom, as a small girl, I belonged. Don't you see? Because of that, I can't bear a story only half told."

"You've managed for about a year!" he said roughly.

"I've been trying to push it back, to crowd other things on top of it. But having to return to Heron House, and now receiving this letter is like a challenge. It's as though something is saying: 'Go on, you *nearly* know!' And I've got to know now, Philip! If by goading whoever sent me that letter into talking too much, then perhaps we'll find out the truth."

"And you'll get hurt —"

"Only for a little while. And since I'm the only one who wants to find out who killed Marcus, then *I'll* pay the temporary price. It's as simple as that!"

Leonie stopped, amazed at herself. She had entered the room shaken and frightened; but she had talked herself into calmness; had faced the facts and emerged with her resolve.

"And you think the police will be able to trace the whispers and the hints?" he exploded. "Must you be such a little fool? Whispers shoot up like weeds from underground and you can go on probing, but you never quite get to the source."

"If and when the time comes," she said quietly, "I shall have faith in the police."

She reached out to take the letter from his desk. Philip's fingers came down like rods on her wrist and held her hand hard against the edge of the table.

"What's the use of coming to see me if you won't take my advice?" he almost shouted at her.

"I'm sorry. I had to tell someone and I hoped, Philip, I did so hope that you would agree with what I'd decided to do!" She got up, as he dropped his hand from her wrist and moved across the room.

Philip watched her and his expression softened.

"Oh Leonie, what am I going to do with you?"

Love me, she wanted to say, *oh, Philip, love me.* . . . Instead she just stood there quietly.

He came close to her and put his hands on her shoulders.

"I want to take you away from it all; away from them all!" his voice was low, urgent. "I want to marry you."

She closed her eyes and involuntarily raised her face to his and felt his lips touch hers, press and harden as he held her close.

"I *will* marry you, Leonie," he said softly, "but leave it to me, darling. I'll have to do things in the way I think right, in my own time. Not to-day, not to-morrow. But one day —"

Yet, as Leonie left the building, she knew that such a promise was not his to give. It was a triangle and there was Claire's place in it to be considered. For all that there was no legal bond, her hold over Philip was subtle and strong. Someone was going to get hurt . . . A little wind danced, warm and sweet with approaching summer, but Leonie shivered as she walked along in the sun.

When she arrived back that evening, the family were collected in the living-room. Old Venetia wore her favourite dark green with amethysts and diamonds gleaming against the high neck of her dress and on her thin, expressive hands. She was looking towards the window where the evening fell in amber and gold on to the quiet trees.

"I really must find another gardener!" The words were spoken against the faint rustle of Leonie's dress as she joined the group. The old eyes remained gazing out of the window, her head did not turn even to acknowledge Leonie. It was as though she were absorbed in her own problem. "Julian," she continued as no one spoke, "you will make some inquiries for me to-morrow."

Leonie glanced at Fran seated on the wide settee and saw the faint stiffening motion of her body.

Julian asked doubtfully. "Do you think you'll get anyone as good as he? After all, Marcus was probably very fussy about his garden and he employed him for ten years —"

"I want someone full-time because I need

him also for a part-time chauffeur." She turned her gaze from the window and looked at them all. "Jim divides his time too much between here and Kew Gardens."

"I'd drive you around, Grandmother," Fran said a little breathlessly.

Venetia gave a faintly impatient chuckle. "My dear child, I want a man at the wheel of my car, and someone I pay a wage to."

"But Grandmother —"

"Let's have no argument! Julian, you will get a list of some good agencies to-morrow." Her voice and her manner were final. "You know my requirements. I want a chauffeur-gardener, full time."

"What you want," Fran said violently, "is to get rid of Jim because you don't like children around! The chauffeur-gardener idea is just an excuse."

"I beg your pardon?" The white head lifted a little; shrewd, pale eyes should have withered Fran. But her young face was burning, her eyes blazed.

"You want to turn a man out of his home, you want to worry and harass him because he's a widower with two children! *Why?* You can scarcely hear Gay and Chris playing from this distance and you don't object to the traffic up the Hill which never seems to stop!"

"Fran, pull yourself together!"

"I know quite well what the trouble is!" Fran stormed on. "Jim's cottage and garden are his own and out of your control, that's what you don't like, isn't it? You don't understand, you don't *want* to understand anyone else's feelings or circumstances. Jim's worked loyally and well here! All this time, while the house has been empty and Diana has been paying him to look after a garden nobody ever came to see or to praise, he went on doing his best, accepting the fact that there was nobody to take an interest. He *cares* about this garden, Grandmother. It's his life! And you're taking it away from him!" She was trembling so that she set her glass down with such force that a little of the sherry spilt.

Hilda rushed to get a cloth; Julian took the glass and wiped it and held it, looking helplessly at the quivering, furious Fran.

Old Venetia watched them with a curious, impersonal gaze though this were a scene from a not very good play.

Then she said:

"Have you quite finished, Fran?"

"No, I haven't! You're my grandmother and this is your house and I've no right to say all this — or rather, *you* think I haven't! *I* think I have. I hate injustice; I hate the power that money gives to crush those who —"

"My dear Fran, you talk like a Dickens character! I'm not crushing anyone, I'm not using my money as a power. All I'm doing is telling you all that I want a man who can give me full-time here."

"Perhaps Jim would if you asked him."

"I prefer to have a change. After all, I'm paying the piper, I have a right to call the tune. And if you imagine Jim is going to walk the streets with two starving children in tow, let me remind you that — little as I know of England — this is a Welfare State. I happen to have heard that he's wanted full time at Kew. You know it, too."

"I know also that he needs to work most of his time near his home because of the children."

"Then let him marry again. Other men do." Her fingers tapped impatiently on the arm of her chair. "And now, let's have no more of this nonsense! You're being very tiresome and utterly childish! I shall expect you to apologise."

Fran looked at her, brow furrowed: "Why did I ever hope you'd understand? After all, you're my grandmother but I scarcely know you! All these years you've been a sort of legend to us over here; you never wrote, you never seemed to remember us — "

"When a continent and two generations separate people there is nothing to write about. Hilda — " her voice rose, "when you've stopped dabbing that table like a nervous housemaid will you go and tell Boadicea to serve dinner as soon as possible?"

Venetia was on her feet. She walked quite steadily to the door, but every movement had an imperious anger. Hilda, scarlet-faced, almost ran out of the room. Julian followed Venetia into the dining-room.

Fran was watching Leonie.

"Go on in to dinner, Leonie! Go and pay lip-service to Grandmother Venetia Sarat!"

"Fran, don't be like this! After all, as she says, she has a right to choose the people she wants to work for her, and it isn't her fault that Jim hasn't a wife to look after the children."

"But it *is* her fault!" Fran cried. "Marcus had *her* blood, *her* imperiousness, her characteristics, and so she's as much to blame as he! If he had never interfered, mocked and sneered, Jim and I would be married and I wouldn't be here now in this house that seems to stand on tip-toe waiting for something — something horrible, to happen!" She turned her back on Leonie, took a cigarette from the box on the low table and lit it with shaking hands. "I'm

173

facing the truth, Leonie. *I'm* the odd-one-out here; you and Julian, like Grandmother, are career people. It's success that you want most. I don't. I want a husband and children; I don't care if I never put on an evening dress again in my whole life; I don't care if I have to spend a quarter of my days at a kitchen sink. All right! I'm ordinary and Jim's ordinary. There's nothing ordinary here! That's why I hate this house. And − I hate Grandmother."

"Don't be silly," Leonie said sharply, "of course you don't!"

"You may think she's just an old lady living still in dreams of grandeur. I tell you, she's more alive than any of us; she's watching us all − there's something going on in that mind of hers, something she's determined to find out. Perhaps after all I'm glad Jim will soon be away from it all! At least then she won't be able to − to −" Fran stopped, drew a little shuddering breath and, in a flash, rushed out of the room.

Leonie remained where she was. Her emotions as she stood in that brilliantly-lit room with the gold and the ormolu and the crimson, were mostly subjective. Fran had said: "It's success you want most!" Here again was a glaring example of how wrong people could be about one another. "You don't want a family," Fran inferred, "a husband and children; you want the limelight, the applause!" Oh Philip, Philip. . . .

She put her hands to her face in a moment's involuntary gesture. How wrong could people be about one another?

Then, how wrong could she be about Fran? The gentle, the warm-hearted cousin, turned suddenly into a virago of shaking fury. And in a mood like that, burning with indignation; seeing everything subjective, as it concerned herself and the man she loved, what was Fran capable of doing? Again it occurred to her that behind the anger there was Fran's love that would be fearless for herself, but fearful for those she loved. For Jim . . . ! Again there came the strong impression that Fran, too, was more involved in the past of a year ago than she had ever admitted.

Leonie pushed the thought away from her and heard Venetia call her impatiently from the dining-room.

Fran was not there, nor did she appear that night. From her position at the head of the table, Venetia seemed to have wiped away all thought of the scene in the living-room. She talked, brightly and amusingly, about her plans for the house; about her life in the States; she ate heartily and, later, in the living-room again, demanded brandy with her coffee.

Perhaps, Leonie thought, watching her with grudging admiration, the secret of her hold on her vitality lay in her ability to wash out anything she did not want to remember, to live in the moment, without doubting the wisdom or regretting anything she had done or said.

X

It was nearly nine o'clock that evening when the telephone bell rang and Leonie, coming downstairs, crossed the hall to answer it.

Philip was on the line.

"Leonie? I hoped you might answer. Will you do something for me? And by the way, be careful what you say on the telephone."

"Yes," she said. " 'Yes' to both those questions."

"Good girl! Then try to find out if there is a typewriter in the house."

"There always used to be one. It was —"

"No," he interrupted quickly. "Let me say it! *You* just say 'Yes' or 'No.' I seem to remember; the typewriter used to be in the alcove off the music-room?"

"Yes."

"Can you manage to get in there and, if you can find that machine, type a few lines — about any old thing. You know — 'The quick brown fox jumps over the lazy dog.' Then I'll have all the letters of the alphabet

177

to check the typewritten envelope."

"I'll do that."

"And ring me to-morrow when you come to town for rehearsal."

"I'll do that, too."

"Oh, and by the way, if you don't find the typewriter in the alcove, it might be up in the attic. I suppose there *is* an attic at Heron House?"

"Yes, a very large one, Philip. It —"

"Uh-uh! No names!" he cautioned. "Good-bye, my darling." The last two words were barely a whisper but as he rang off they seemed to sing inside her, filling her being.

Turning away from the telephone, she saw her grandmother coming along the passage. She walked without hesitating past Leonie and went into the living-room. As she did so, she asked:

"Did Philip want Claire?"

"No."

"But it *was* Philip on the telephone, wasn't it? I heard you mention his name."

"Yes, it was."

"Well? I was in the kitchen with Boadicea if he was ringing me on business —" She was standing just inside the door, looking at Leonie.

"Philip only wanted a word with me."

"Come along into the room, child. Don't stand in the doorway like a tradesman!" She watched Leonie enter and perch on the arm of a chair. "So Philip was ringing *you!* It's a good thing it was only I who came along at that moment and not Claire, isn't it?" the old eyes were very bright.

"My talk with Philip wasn't – wasn't just a pleasant little chat! I mean –"

"He didn't ring you up to give you his love? Is that what you mean?" Old Venetia chuckled. "I should hope he didn't." She waited as though expecting an explanation.

Leonie leaned over and took a chocolate from a box and began to eat it.

"Claire *has* been here before. Had you any idea?"

The unexpected switch in the trend of the conversation startled Leonie.

"You asked me that before, Grandmother, and I said I didn't know."

"In the meantime have you tried to find out?"

"No." She swallowed the chocolate and coughed a little with its over-sweetness.

"Then talk to her. She may give herself away to you. She won't to me. Excitement took her off her guard the other day when she mentioned those special lights Marcus had and which I only knew about because I found them in the attic. But she'll be more cautious from now on! Her own revelation shook her, though she covered it up as well as she could."

"Even if she has been here before, she may want to forget all about it because of what happened. Surely it isn't important!"

Old Venetia didn't seem to hear her. She was picking at the strap of her big black crocodile handbag, muttering to herself.

"How well did Claire know Marcus? And just when? Towards the end of his life? And if so — yes, it could have been Claire!"

"What could?"

The white head lifted; the pale eyes lost their inward look.

"Nothing! Nothing at all! I was wandering a little, that is all."

"No Grandmother, you don't wander!" Leonie spoke firmly. "You were thinking aloud, perhaps. And you said you wondered just when Claire had known Marcus. It seems to trouble you and if that's so, why not let her go? Make an excuse, say you want her room for some relative and let her go back to her flat."

"No." Her voice was strong and final. "No, Leonie. I want Claire here. I am curious and I want to know what she is hiding."

An old woman's whim? A bright, inquisitive

mind with little to expend its energy on except the doings of those around her? Leonie wondered – and tried to tell herself that that was all it was.

Julian came into the room and Leonie escaped with the plea of chores, nylons to wash, shoes to clean. . . .

She knew that she could not try to find Marcus's typewriter to-night, even if it were still in the house. Old people wandered at night. Venetia might come downstairs and find her there. Or Julian, returning from working late in his studio. The morning would be the best time, when no lights were needed in the music-room and everyone was busy about their jobs.

Leonie was getting ready for bed when Fran came in. She knew, as she heard her pass her door, that she could not go to her. Their friendship was broken because neither was quite able to trust the other any more. In the past there had been an in-tuneness between them. Now that was gone and each had their own secret emotions; each thought the other could not understand. Leonie knew she could not tell Fran about Philip lest by a word or a glance she unwittingly betrayed the secret to others in the house. And Fran's love for Jim was something that both puzzled and troubled

Leonie. For some reason or other, behind whatever misunderstandings they might have between them as to whether or not they could get married, Fran's fear for him was connected with Marcus's death.

Suppose Jim had quarrelled with Marcus over Fran? Suppose he had picked up the little stone cat in the violence of sudden temper and flung it at Marcus, not meaning to kill – just in blind rage. And suppose Fran knew? Being Fran and understanding, she might love him the more for his tragic defence of her. Suppose a witness had perjured himself on Jim's behalf: "I saw him myself in one of the glass-houses at Kew that night." And suppose Fran, knowing it, had lost her head and fled to South America?

Conjecture on conjecture! Where could it lead but into a labyrinth of suspicions, reaching out to ensnare every one of them?

Leonie lay, straight and still in bed and tried to stop her thoughts. Eyes closed, she focused her attention on her part in the play; saying her lines, visualizing the second act which held a difficult scene for her.

She had no idea whether she really fell asleep or only dozed. But suddenly something seeped into her mind. She opened her eyes and sat up with a start. Somewhere, outside the room –

in the passage or in the garden – she had heard music – singing or humming or whistling – she had been too near real sleep to be certain which.

But she recognised the unusual arrangement of notes in a minor key! She listened, her heart beating hard. There was no sound, no trees stirring in the wind, no car passing up Richmond Hill. The night outside the windows was pitch black and as moveless as a picture post-card.

Had she dreamed that bar or so, once so hauntingly familiar – the theme music of the concerto Marcus had been working on when he was killed . . . ? The curiously-beautiful, lonely, pagan sound Marcus had said would be introduced into the concerto by the *cor anglais.*

She got up and went, feeling her way in the darkness, to the window. There was a light far away in Jim's cottage, but nobody moved down the dark garden.

She must have dreamt those few strange notes. Yet if so, why had she wakened? She went back to bed shivering in the chill midnight, and found herself lying tense and listening, though she knew that she would not hear the sound again. Either it *had* been her own dream, or someone had passed beneath the window humming or whistling Marcus's theme music.

When Marcus was at his piano, he would keep his windows closed, summer and winter. He hated unseen audiences and Jim was never allowed to work near the house at those times. That was the reason there were merely shrubs and lawns close to the walls, with the flower gardens below the small terrace. Jim could not, therefore, have heard the theme music since, even had he come to the house for Florrie's "elevenses," the baize door would have blocked out the sounds from the music-room. Florrie might have heard the music at such times that she had to disturb him because of a telephone call, a telegram or a cable. But Florrie was hundreds of miles away. Anyway, Marcus had only found the theme for his concerto in the last few days of his life. Who then, among the people now in the house, had been there a year ago. No one here had admitted it. The more Leonie thought about it, the more certain she was that she had not dreamed the music.

It was not music easily remembered; yet it had so haunted someone that twelve whole months later they hummed it in the dark.

Had Fran been at the house, storming at Marcus for his mockery of her love? Or Jim when he had walked in, defiant and angry, upon Marcus? Who else could have been there? Claire? Old Venetia was certain that she had known Marcus better than she pretended. Or was there still another person, a fourth man, a fourth woman?

But why should some outsider stalk through the gardens at midnight? Because there was someone here dangerous to him or to her and this humming of the music was another deliberate warning. . . .

Suddenly Leonie felt that she had hit upon the answer. Someone was haunting *her*, watching *her!* If she told anyone about it they would merely say, "You dreamed it!" But the more she thought about it, the more certain she was that it had been no dream.

And then another thought occurred to her. There were telephone extensions in the house. Had someone lifted a receiver when Philip called her to-night, and heard him ask her to find Marcus's typewriter? It strengthened her conviction that this was just another way to try to frighten her into leaving things alone.

XI

Soon after breakfast the next day, Leonie tried the door of the music-room. Both were locked, and Venetia had the keys.

She walked back from the garden door remembering that Diana had sold the house as it stood with everything in it. Old Venetia had rid herself of most of Marcus's possessions because they were most certainly not her taste. But she would probably not have bothered about oddments in the attic. There was a possibility, then, that the typewriter had found its way up there. Since she could not get into the music-room, she might at least have a look there this morning.

On the first landing, Leonie saw Hilda through the open doorway of her room, busy making her bed. She slipped past her, past Boadicea singing in the bathroom in a rich contralto, full of the sonorous nostalgia of her race, "Am goin' to de Lord!" and sloshing water round the bath. Leonie reached the narrow staircase that led to the attic. She went quickly up. There was an old table by the window and on it, as though waiting for her, stood the typewriter. Quickly she took the piece of paper she had brought with her and typed the sentence Philip had suggested three times. Then she covered the typewriter and went to the door of the room and listened.

Everything on the immediate landing below was quiet. She went down the first few steep stairs and then checked her step.

The fanlight over old Venetia's bedroom was open and her voice, trained by long years on the stage to carry, struck out clearly and angrily.

"Then you must talk to Claire. Find out!"

"I wish you'd never asked her here." It was Julian with her, his voice protesting and unhappy.

"Well, I did, and I'm certainly not going to let her leave before I know what she knows! Don't be a fool, Julian!"

"That's all very well, but I've a feeling she's dangerous!"

"Of course she's dangerous! People with small, secretive faces always are!"

"You said when Leonie brought the subject up on her first evening, that you wanted it closed. You said —"

"I'm not senile, I remember precisely what I

said," Venetia snapped. "But things have changed. I've had intuitions all my life, and they don't usually let me down. I believe Claire knew Marcus very well. I believe she's been trying to hide from us just how well she knew him, and I intend to find out!"

"You think — she could have been here on that night —?"

"The night Marcus was killed?" old Venetia could say the words Julian hesitated over. "She might well have been."

"*Claire?* It could have been — Claire —?"

"We must find out, mustn't we?"

"No. Venetia, leave it! You said, 'What's done is done!' Leave it that way!"

There was a pause. Then:

"Oh go! *Go!* You make me tired!"

"But, Venetia, you're not being consistent! First you want it forgotten, now you're playing with it like a cat with a mouse. And I know it could be dangerous!"

"So are many things I've done in my life! And if I choose to change my mind, that's my affair. Now I want to get up. Call Boadicea for me. And don't look as though devils were after you. Nobody's going to harm you!"

The door opened so quickly that Leonie had only just time to draw back.

When Julian had vanished down the main

staircase, Leonie slipped along the corridor to her own room.

If Claire was here on the night that Marcus was killed. . . .

But she couldn't have been or the police would have found out. If, however, they never even knew that she was friendly with Marcus, why should they question her?

Leonie folded the sheet of typing paper and put it in her handbag, glanced at her watch and found that she would be late if she didn't hurry.

To her secret dismay she found Julian in the drive with the engine of his car running.

"I'm going to town again. Leonie. I'll run you up to the theatre."

There was no excuse she could give. She murmured her thanks and let him settle her in the passenger seat. Then, when he got in behind the wheel and the car slid forward she glanced back at the house. Old Venetia was standing at a tall landing window watching them. Leonie couldn't see from this distance, but she was quite certain that she was smiling. . . .

In the car, Julian was at first very quiet. It was as though he were unsure of himself as far as she was concerned after the night in the garden, as though he were waiting for her to make the first friendly advance. As they were crossing Hammersmith Bridge, however, he broke the difficult silence.

"I'm sorry, Leonie, about the other night."

"Let's forget it, shall we?" She stared ahead of her at the silver ribbon of the Thames flowing swiftly, sparkling in the sunlight.

"And forgive?"

"Of course — only, don't do it again! I don't like having to fight a man off!"

"Some women love it!" he said with a faint smile. "They collect scalps."

"Well, I don't!"

"Subject dropped and forgotten!" he said lightly. "Let's talk about — what?"

She was grateful for his good-tempered acceptance.

"There are a few million subjects to choose from."

"There *is* one thing —"

"What?" her voice was cautious.

"Your cousin, Fran. I like her, she's pretty and charming. But she's like a cat walking along wires! You don't see her much because you aren't at the house, but she has got something on her mind and Grandmother notices it. They don't like each other, you know!"

"Fran's had a lot to do with young people

and I think she feels that Grandmother is a bit inclined to be impatient with Jim's children."

"It's odd. Venetia used to like young people around her – out in New Orleans they adored her. But since she's been here she's changed. In fact, this house seems to have changed us all!"

"Give everyone time to settle down."

"Time won't help, Leonie. Only one thing will –"

"What's that?"

"If someone burned Heron House to the ground!"

He spoke so vehemently that she turned quickly and looked at him. His face was grave and angry, his hands were tight on the wheel as though he wanted to grip the life out of it.

She said defensively. "It's a beautiful house – it was my home."

"But things have happened there which have made it evil!"

"You don't blame a house for the actions of people who have lived there. And anyway, no one in the house killed Marcus, because there was only Florrie living in, and she couldn't hurt a spider. *I know!*"

Suddenly Julian reached out and touched her hand, lightly. He said:

"Once again – subject dropped and forgotten, eh, Leonie?"

"I wish you would," she said urgently.

"Let's talk of the theatre."

"Yes, let's," she said with relief. "Did you know that they're bringing that new American musical *Cabbages and Kings* to London sometime in the autumn?"

Conversation flowed now, happily and impersonally, until Julian set her down at the theatre.

The rehearsal that morning was tricky because of alterations to the script. When, at half past one, they broke for lunch, Leonie took a taxi to Philip's office and gave the envelope containing the paper on which she had taken a specimen of the typewriter in the attic, to the receptionist to be handed to him. There was also a note from her telling him that she would be at her flat late that afternoon.

He telephoned her there.

"Disappointing news, Leonie! The type doesn't tally!"

"I never thought it would. I told you, I don't believe that note is as naïve as it seems. Whoever sent it had only to go into any big store, say they were thinking of buying a machine, try some typewriters, using envelopes of their own on various machines and then leave, promising to call again. One envelope was used; the rest destroyed. At least that's how I see it could have been done if whoever sent the note didn't want the typewriter traced."

"And I still mayn't hand it to the police?"

"No."

"You're a self-willed, crazy little chump! But one thing I am going to do, whether you like it or not. *I'm* keeping this note locked up in my safe here."

"I wish you would. I'd hate to have it around, and I suppose it must be kept."

"You're dead right, it must!"

Walking up the drive of Heron House that evening in the bright sunlight, Leonie found Venetia wandering between the flower beds.

She had time to watch her before Venetia saw her. Seen in the soft afternoon light, she was just an old lady walking among her flowers. The house stood bathed in sunlight, its windows open. Julian's repaired car stood in the drive. Birds sang.

The whole scene was so normal, so beautiful that it did not seem possible that the shadow of violence still hung over the house. Nor did it seem anything but incongruous that someone so hated and feared Leonie that they wanted her out of the house.

Her grandmother saw her and beckoned. Leonie crossed the lawn and joined her.

"I'm going to have more rose trees planted," old Venetia explained. "I thought these two beds here —" she went forward, leading Leonie with a hand on her arm, to a space outside the music-room. "What I would really like would be oleanders — I grew them in New Orleans, but I suppose they wouldn't flourish here." She stopped, raised her head and asked: "What's that?"

They listened together. Clearly and plaintively came the mewing of a cat.

"It's Livvy —" Leonie began.

The mewing was coming from the music-room.

Venetia's expression changed. The benign look had gone.

"Hilda's cat! How did it get in there? But there's no need to ask! Even her idiotic fear that the house is haunted doesn't stop her probing and prying — though heaven knows what she expects to find!"

"Hadn't we better let the cat out?"

"Yes, of course," she turned to Leonie. "You will find my bag in my bedroom. Get the key. It's a large one, rather — ornate — but then you know it, don't you? And if you see Hilda, tell her I want her."

Leonie found the key, but she made no attempt to look for Hilda.

When the garden door was open, the little cat shot past them, bounding into the sun, tail erect.

"What did Hilda want here?" Old Venetia was wandering round the room. She scrutinised everything and then went into the large alcove with its books of music. The place was empty and nothing had been disarranged.

"I wouldn't be surprised," her grandmother was saying, returning to the music-room, "if she wasn't having a good look round prior to suggesting that she and Julian might have this room for their private sitting-room. She probably came in to see if her jittery nerves could stand it!"

Leonie was still in the alcove. Now that she was here she saw her chance to find out if there was another typewriter – she seemed to remember that there had been a very ancient one and it had not been up in the attic.

She moved round, bending to open the cupboards under the bookshelves.

"I shouldn't bother," old Venetia's faintly sarcastic voice came from the arch between the two rooms. "I don't imagine even Hilda, small as she is, could hide in a cupboard!"

Leonie took no notice. There was only one more little door to open. She opened it. There was no typewriter there.

"Leonie! What's the matter with you?"

She watched her granddaughter rejoin her and said, looking round:

"I'm planning to move Marcus's things out of here and sell them. Then I shall have the room completely redecorated and re-furnished," she walked to the desk and ran her hands along the rich dark top, looked at her finger and said, "Dust! I must get Boadicea to come in." Still looking at her finger, she went on: "Give up your flat, Leonie."

Leonie, startled at the sudden change of conversation, asked:

"But why? I like my little flat."

"It's probably small and pokey. Come here and live with me. You shall have this room for yourself, to entertain your own friends in – I would change its appearance so much, my dear, that you wouldn't recognise it. You'd manage to forget what had happened in it."

"I couldn't do that –"

"What nonsense! When you've had plenty of knocks in life you'll learn not to be so sensitive! It's a foolish trait! Come here, Leonie. I would love it and it would be good for Julian to have someone he can talk to – someone of the theatre."

"I fought hard for my independence, Grandmother. I can't give it up."

The strange, light-gold eyes watched her.

"Think it over. Never make hasty decisions," she turned her head quickly, hearing footsteps, and went to the garden door. "Hilda! Is that Hilda?"

"Yes —" Obedient as a child, Hilda came towards them.

"What were you doing in the music-room?"

"Me? In there?" Hilda stammered. "I don't know what you mean!"

"I always mean precisely what I say."

"But I haven't been near it! Why should I? I don't want to see that beastly room!"

"Your cat was in there."

"Livvy? So that's where she got to! I've been looking for her everywhere. But how did she get in?"

"That's what *I'm* asking you!"

Leonie slipped away. If Hilda was to be humiliated, then at least she wouldn't have to bear an audience.

XII

When she had washed and done her hair, Leonie went down again and into the garden. No one was about and she made for a wrought-iron seat on the lawn facing the sun.

She had to pass the music-room on her way. No one stood outside now. Whatever Venetia and Hilda had said to one another was over. The only sounds were the birds' songs and the distant traffic on Richmond Hill and a soft hammering which must be coming from the studio where Julian was still at work.

But directly she sat down, Leonie knew that the hammering wasn't coming from there. She turned her head in its direction.

Someone was in the music-room, knocking to be let out. And this time it wasn't the little cat. . . .

She went quickly to the closed door.

"Is anyone there?"

She peered in and the room seemed empty. Then she heard a voice which came from the thick folds of the curtains.

"I can't open this door. Let me out!" the voice was too smothered to be recognisable.

"I haven't got a key. Go to the window in the alcove and open it." She went quickly round the side of the house and saw, as she glanced in, Claire's round face at the window.

Reaching up, she flung the window open, measuring the distance from the floor to the sill.

"But I can't climb up there! I'll have to have help –" Claire cried.

"All right. I'll come in." Leonie hoisted herself on to the sill and dropped down into the room.

For a moment she gazed at Claire. "So it was you who let Hilda's little cat in!"

"I didn't know I did! I happened to find the key to one of these doors on the hall table. It didn't fit the house door, so I tried this."

"How did you know it was one of the keys to the music-room?"

"Oh, I saw your grandmother with it one day," Claire answered readily. "Anyway, I got the door open, put the key back and then – well, I just came in. I didn't know that wretched little cat had pushed its way in, too!"

"But why did you go to all that trouble to see this room?"

"My dear Leonie, it's a perfectly harmless

thing to want to do surely!"

Something in Claire's lofty superciliousness goaded Leonie.

"Small children are intrigued by locked doors, but I didn't think adults found them irresistible!"

"Why all these questions, Leonie?"

"Would you like Grandmother to ask them?"

"Are you threatening me? Are you hinting that you'll tell her?"

"She thinks Hilda has been in here and she's never very kind to her. I don't see why she should be made the scapegoat for something she didn't do."

"Oh, what a fuss to make!"

"Maybe! But Grandmother doesn't want anyone in this room until she has had it entirely redecorated and furnished. I think that's feasible enough — and anyway, it's her house, you know!"

"If you're trying to remind me of my manners, I'd like to explain that your grandmother said: 'Make this your home until you go into hospital.' And I'm interested in all the rooms in my home!"

"What were you looking for here?"

"You wouldn't understand professional inquisitiveness, would you, Leonie? Everyone told me how beautiful this room was and, being an interior decorator, I wanted to see for myself. That's the simple truth."

"By the way, where were you when Grandmother and I came in a little while ago and let the cat out?"

Claire smiled. "Hidden behind the curtains, making myself as flat as possible and thankful that I'm small!"

Nothing could shake that supreme self-confidence! Leonie said impatiently:

"Let's go. But you'll have to climb through the window. I'll help you."

Claire glanced at her wrist-watch.

"Your grandmother will be in the drawing-room now with her cocktail. I heard Julian go past a little while ago, so he'll be there too. There's no one to hear us −"

"Maybe not, but *I* don't want to stay here!"

Claire was frowning a little. She said slowly:

"Since everyone is shut up in the house, we may as well talk here."

"I'm going −"

"Leonie, please stay!" Claire's arm reached out and barred the window. "I've got a question I want to ask you."

Leonie walked to the bookshelves, deliberately turning her back on Claire. She looked down and saw a pile of volumes bound in red morocco lying on the wide shelf above the built-in cupboards. She thought vaguely that these finely-bound volumes hadn't been there in Marcus's day. . . .

"I asked you, Leonie," Claire was repeating with exaggerated patience: "Why did Philip ring you up last night?"

Leonie swung round in dismay.

"Who told you he did?"

"Your grandmother."

"Oh no!"

"Oh yes!" Claire nodded. "In fact, she was most concerned. You know what she said? 'Hold on tight to that young man of yours. He's charming. Don't lose him!' I told her there was no fear of that. Your grandmother is so wise, and so just! You may be a blood-relation, but it was me she was concerned about!"

Leonie's fingers lifted the heavy cover of the top volume on the shelf and saw that they were scrap books, pasted thickly with photographs and printed matter.

"Leonie, are you listening?"

"I don't want to. I want to get out of here before someone comes and finds us. If you won't let me help you out, then I shall have to go and ask for the key to let you out the door."

Claire moved. "Very well. We can talk some-where else. I want an answer, you know, Leonie."

It wasn't easy helping someone you were beginning to hate! But Leonie fetched a chair, almost lifting Claire on to it and then twisting through the window herself in order to help her down on the other side. Claire was making it all as difficult as she could, but as she half-pulled, half-lifted her, Leonie was letting her thoughts work on in their own way.

Old Venetia had been serving her own ends by warning Claire to keep her hold on Philip. Nothing must go wrong with this long-term plan of hers, this devouring dream that one day Julian would be free of Hilda and Leonie would be waiting for him. . . .

The two girls stood on the path below the window. Claire was smoothing down her skirt; there was an expression of pain in her eyes.

"I'm sorry if I had to hurt you —" Leonie began.

"Oh, you couldn't help it." She glanced over her shoulder. "Hadn't you better shut that window?"

Leonie pulled it up as closely as she could. "It will have to be locked from the inside, sometime. Come along let's get into the house."

Claire was leaning a little against the wall. Her face was as pale as the magnolia flowers behind her.

"We haven't finished talking. You see, I think we'd both better know where we stand — with regard to Philip, I mean."

"I don't want to talk about Philip."

"I'm sure you don't. But you'll have to listen, because *I* want to talk to *you!* This is something important, Leonie, and it's got to be said. You must realise that it's been hard for Philip all this time. First I had that horrible accident and now I'm faced with this operation and then with divorcing Johnnie. It's a lot to ask a man to put up with and when two people have to wait for each other a long time, it imposes a terrific strain, especially on the man." She paused.

"You don't have to tell me all this."

"Oh, but I think I do." Claire picked a glossy magnolia leaf, pulling it apart. "You see, Leonie, I know that you're in love with Philip."

"I'm going —"

"I shouldn't. Not till I've finished what I want to say, because it's terribly important to the three of us. I love Philip, too. And I don't want him to get hurt." She dropped the torn leaf and her eyes, dark and burning in her pale face, looked steadily at Leonie. "That's why I must talk to you and warn you."

"If you — love Philip — talk to *him* about —

anything you have – to say –"

"But Leonie," Claire's voice was curiously without violence, "I want to try and explain myself to you so that you'll understand. You see, I know how easily my love could change to hate. If Philip hurt me or let me down, I'd hurt him back far, far more! Lots of people want to hurt hard when they've had their hope and happiness taken away from them, but most of them haven't the courage. *I* have!" the voice went on softly, as though walking on tiptoe through her words. "Believe me, I can't bear the thought that I could hurt Philip – but I know I would if anyone took him from me."

It was curious, but Leonie couldn't move; she couldn't walk away. There was something hypnotic in that sweet reasonableness, something horrible, something frightening – a twisted power that could turn from good to evil.

"Philip *does* love me, you know!" the terrible, gentle voice went on. "But it's been such a long time, this waiting, and however fond two people are of one another, there are times when the relationship tends to get a bit stale. That's when people like you, Leonie, attractive and with the glamour of the stage behind you, can ruin everything. *Don't* – don't even try!"

Leonie turned quickly, finding power of

movement at last.

But Claire was quicker. She stood in her path and, with the bushes on either side of her, made a barrier.

"Philip has his profession, his living to think of," Claire went on. "When I divorce Johnnie, I shall be the innocent party and everything will be all right. But it would be quite another matter if I took Philip to court. I could ruin him, you know. Or rather, indirectly, it would be *you* who would ruin him!"

"Philip has done nothing that could bring him into the courts!" Leonie cried.

"There's such a thing as breach of promise."

"As you're already married, that can't apply."

"But you don't know the facts, and I think you should. Johnnie left me —"

"Yes, so I heard."

"But you don't know the rest, do you? He came back not so very long ago and wanted us to try and make a success of our marriage. I told him about Philip — I said that, because of him, there could be no hope of a reconcilation."

"But if Johnnie wants to come back to you," Leonie said, "you can't divorce him for desertion, can you?"

Claire was tearing at another beautiful, shining magnolia leaf.

"That's just it. In fact, Leonie, I had to bribe Johnnie to stay away and agree to be divorced. I promised to settle money on him if he would let himself be divorced – and I did it with Philip's connivance."

"I don't believe it! Philip wouldn't –"

"What you believe or don't believe doesn't come into it!" Claire said brutally. "*I* say, and I shall go on saying, that Philip knows perfectly well the lengths to which I'm going to get free of Johnnie – for him!"

"You can't involve him like this – Claire, you wouldn't dare!"

Claire's eyes flicked over Leonie. "For a sophisticated actress, you're being almost naïve. I told you that when I got hurt, I hurt back. In a court of law it would be my word against Philip's. If, when I am free of Johnnie, Philip let me down – then he will know what to expect. And believe me, *I'll* stir the courts to compassion; *I'll* work on their emotions! Philip Drew, who encouraged me to bribe Johnnie, to get free of him because he said *he* loved me; Philip who pursued me! I'll do so much damage to his career, Leonie, if I lose him, that I'll be almost sorry for him myself."

"You'll do damage to yourself, too!"

"Oh, that won't matter! I'll get over it in time. It's Philip who never will!"

Way back in the house, Boadicea was beating the gong.

"I'm not the daughter of a lawyer for nothing, Leonie. I know ways in which I can harm Philip —" Leonie was staring at her. She had her hands held tightly together in front of her because, if she relaxed, she felt she would hit Claire.

"You make me utterly sick!" she said at last very quietly and pushed past her with her shoulder so roughly that Claire staggered. Leonie didn't turn round; she marched up the path and into the house.

It was Venetia who said that Claire had gone into town to dine with Philip that evening. Leonie, drinking sherry, thought it tasted like vinegar and knew that it was the very finest Bristol Cream.

It was on the tip of her tongue to say: "It was Claire not Hilda, in the music-room." But she didn't; she just said nothing and knew that her courage was a frozen thing.

She couldn't sleep that night. She knew, now, without a doubt that Claire had been watching them on that first night of her arrival at Heron House and had seen how close they were, how earnestly they spoke. She probably believed that Hilda had spoken the truth on the night of the car accident and that she had found Philip at Leonie's flat. She most certainly put a wrong construction on the telephone call which old Venetia had overheard!

In the morning, she woke unrefreshed. This was hopeless; she couldn't go through strenuous last rehearsals and the first vital performance of the play if she were subject to the tensions that seemed to surround her here.

As she dressed, she decided that she must go back to her flat, at least for a few days until she felt sufficiently in her part to be able to cope with outside difficulties as well.

But when, after breakfast, she went to Venetia's room she met Boadicea coming out, closing the door softly.

"M's Venetia am feeling tired dis mornin'."

"I was going in to talk to her, but I'd better not, then."

The old negress shook her head. "M's Venetia don't sleep no good. Leastways, not last night."

"Did she say what disturbed her?"

"She sleep light, like old ladies, M's Sarat."

Had Venetia, too, heard someone humming or whistling around midnight? But even if she had and it had disturbed her, she could not have understood its significance.

Later, in the drive, Leonie saw Claire just getting into her little car. She wore a grey dress and a short white coat. Her dark hair was smooth and gleaming in the sunlight.

"Oh, Leonie," she called, "about last evening —"

Anger began to well up inside Leonie.

"You've had your say! I'm in a hurry!"

"You resent my plain-speaking, don't you?"

"I didn't consider it a pleasant little chat, if that's what you mean." She walked past Claire, willing the arrival of the taxi she had ordered.

But Claire limped after her. She had an unusual air of uncertainty as though during the night she had had second thoughts about that impulse that had made her so outspoken.

"All I wanted to do was to get things straight —"

"You did! You left me in no possible doubt!" Leonie's eyes were riveted on the open entrance gates, willing the taxi to come.

"I suppose in a way I've got a masculine mind," Claire mused. "I speak frankly and hope the other person will understand. But women don't, do they? They become offended; they can't take anything straight from the shoulder like a man; they can't even argue without getting angry. In fact, they behave as though truth should be hidden like a hoard of gold!"

"*You* talk about truth? You who – oh, what's the use?" She picked up her case and walked rapidly towards the flung-back gates.

"Are you going away?" Claire called.

Leonie didn't answer. At that moment the taxi swung into the drive, swerved to avoid Leonie, and came to a stop.

"Looks like you got tired of waiting, miss, and started to walk," grinned the taxi man.

Leonie shook her head.

"It's just that I've cut it rather fine. It's not your fault but I'd be grateful if you could – well – step on it a bit –"

"I took you up to the theatre the other day, didn't I? You're Miss Leonie Sarat, aren't you?"

"That's right," she smiled at him and got into the taxi.

"The old bus'll have wings!" said the man. "Here we go!" and roared with a fine sweep out of the drive.

Leonie was perfectly aware that Claire watched her, perhaps a little smilingly because she was undoubted mistress of the situation.

Had Claire really expected her to feel no bitterness, no horror at what she had been told? Perhaps she really did! Perhaps she was one of those people who could find justification in any action she chose to take.

Perhaps she could deal a fatal blow and turn it into a virtue. . . . Deal a fatal blow . . . the kind of blow Marcus had received by an unknown hand! Why remember him at this moment? What was the connection that slid up from her subconscious mind?

Questions that couldn't be answered . . . fears that couldn't be allayed . . . suspicions that couldn't be verified.

And back there, just behind her, a beautiful house held evil — held someone who was waiting, and watching. . . .

XIII

That night, when Leonie arrived back at the house, old Venetia was in the living-room. There was no trace of tiredness about her; she looked, in fact, very alert and angry.

"Have you seen Fran to-day?"

"No. Why?"

"I had quite a morning with her and now, it seems, she has disappeared."

"It's getting late, Grandmother, she'll be back soon."

"That's just it. She won't."

Leonie sat down in one of the deep chairs and looked across at the erect, angry woman, and waited.

"I dismissed Jim this morning," old Venetia said. "I gave him a fortnight's notice and told him that I needed the cottage for a full-time man. He took it perfectly well and said he would try to go in a week's time, and then, if I'd found a full-time man, the cottage would be vacant for him. I had a feeling he was almost glad to go. Sometime later Fran came storming in. She behaved as though I'd done something criminal. Then, after having had her say almost without taking a breath, scarlet faced and like a little fury, she walked out. I haven't seen her since."

"She's probably gone to cool off. Don't worry, Grandmother."

"I sent Boadicea to her room at lunch-time because she hadn't come down. She wasn't there and most of her belongings had gone."

"But surely someone saw her go? Hilda – or Julian?"

"Julian was in his studio all the morning and Hilda went shopping. Boadicea was in the kitchen and I was in my room so that nobody heard the taxi come for her. She must have ordered one because she arrived with two large suitcases." Her shrewd old eyes levelled at Leonie. "You didn't get a call from her to-day?"

"No. I've been at rehearsals."

"You don't think she can have gone to your flat?"

"She couldn't get in, if she did. I've got the keys."

"I gather you were such great friends in the past, according to Fran, that I thought you might know where she might be."

"We haven't seen one another for over a year, Grandmother. People grow apart, you know!"

"Can you make a guess where she's gone? Some close friends?"

Leonie shook her head. "It's too long ago for me to remember who they are. We had no mutual friends even in those days."

"She seems to have neither good manners nor common sense — behaving like a little fish-wife because I sack my gardener!" Venetia snapped. She stirred, rested her beautiful hands on the arms of her chair and helped herself to her feet. "Well, I'm not sitting up half the night because a granddaughter decides to leave my house! Will you tell Boadicea I want her?"

"Yes, of course."

"And if Fran should sufficiently remember her manners to telephone me, will you say I am not to be disturbed?"

Leonie went in search of Boadicea and then let herself out of the house. She was quite certain that Jim would know where Fran was.

In the heavy, clouded night it was not easy to find her way down the paths, but when she reached the hornbeam garden, someone stepped out of the shadows and she gave a little cry of alarm.

"It's all right, Leonie," Julian said. "I've been working so hard that I'm nearly dizzy, so I thought I'd have some fresh air. I never dreamed I'd have company as well!" his hand went out as though to take her hand.

Leonie drew away.

"I'm going down to the cottage to ask Jim if he knows where Fran is. You know she's gone?"

"I do! Venetia is furious. But there's plenty of time for you to see Jim — it's early. Walk down to the terrace with me. I so seldom have you to myself —"

"I'm sorry but I must see Jim! I'm worried about Fran."

"For Pete's sake, she's old enough to look after herself! Let her be! Leonie — let me talk to you!" His words pleaded, but his fingers clung to her arm.

Exasperation, extreme tiredness after an exacting day, irritation that she could not walk in the garden without Juilian dogging her footsteps, made her turn on him.

"Isn't there enough trouble in this house without you making things more difficult?" she cried. "Everyone here, for reasons of their own, is living on the edge of a volcano which could erupt at any moment. And *you* have to complicate matters! Leave me alone — don't come stalking me wherever I go because I've had enough of emotions and tension to last me a life-time!"

"For heaven's sake," he retaliated, "don't blame me for everything that's going on here! I'm as sick of it as you are! I never before believed that houses could be evil, but now I do."

"That's ghoulish nonsense! This house is beautiful and it could be a happy place. Someone in it is ruining everything – someone –"

Julian caught his breath. *"Who?"* he whispered.

"I – I don't know! That's just it. But someone is filling this house with fear."

"Then, Leonie, that's all the more reason why at least two of us should remain close, getting strength from one another. Don't you see, this could be the only way we can live here. You and I –"

"You could stop and give a thought that you're married!"

"To a neurotic little moron! God help me!"

"I don't gather Hilda was that when you married her, so you might start to consider what made her that way."

"I can't help not loving her! Venetia hasn't helped – she'd like me to be free of her. She wants us –"

"Stop hiding behind what Grandmother said!" Leonie cried. "Stop justifying yourself *and leave me alone!*" She flung herself away from him and walked quickly away, relieved that he made no attempt to follow her. It was one thing to pity his weakness, another to encourage him. She knew quite well that her Grandmother could enforce her will upon him so that he came to believe it to be his. But she wouldn't have her footsteps dogged, wouldn't give Hilda cause for suspicion.

When she was clear of the hornbeam garden she saw that there was a light in Jim's sitting-room and almost as soon as she knocked, he opened the door as though he had heard her coming.

"Come in, Miss Sarat." His dark handsome face smiled at her. "I'm in rather a muddle because I'm clearing out — I seem to have collected a lorry-load of rubbish since I've been here."

She followed him into the small, comfortable sitting-room.

"I'm sorry to hear you're leaving, Jim."

"Every employer has a right to choose the staff he or she wants," he said philosophically. He cleared a chair for her. "I've sent the children to my sister's for a week or so while I look round."

"Will you go full-time to Kew now?"

"I may. I don't know." He looked around

218

him at the muddle of toys and old books, letters and photographs that littered the room. "My main problem at the moment is to know what to keep and what to throw away. I'm glad the children aren't here or everything they possess, every bit of string or broken toy, would be kept." He grinned at her. "But children live in the present; they'll forget old books and old dolls. At least, I hope they will because wherever we go there probably won't be as much room for their stuff as there is here."

"Jim, I came here to ask you if you know where Fran is."

His eyes went past her to the uncurtained window. He said evasively:

"Fran hated being here — she didn't realise how it would affect her!"

"But you *do* know where she's gone?"

"Yes."

"Will you tell me?" she asked gently. "I want to go and see her."

"That's difficult! She made me promise not to say." His large brown hands plucked at the stays of a little broken sailing boat he had picked up from the table.

"But in heaven's name, why keep it a secret? What's she afraid of?"

"I suppose that someone will try and persuade her to return."

"Why should they? She's free to go if she wants. She was only staying here as Grandmother's guest, anyway, and I think she might have told her she was leaving."

"I'm sorry, Miss Sarat." He looked unhappy and embarrassed.

"Jim," Leonie leaned forward. "What is Fran afraid of?"

His eyes didn't flinch. "Why should she be afraid of anything?"

"I don't know, but she is. You should know that."

"It's more that she's upset, Miss Sarat. She doesn't quite understand why I have to leave. She thinks her grandmother is just making an excuse to get rid of me."

"Oh no! It's more than that? Hasn't she talked to you about it?"

"About what?" his voice was cautious.

"About the reason she's on edge. Afraid!"

"No! Is she?"

Silence hung between them, awkward, filled with their own secret thoughts. Then Leonie took hold of her courage.

"Do you love Fran?"

"Yes."

"Then why don't you marry her?"

His face darkened; his eyes looked at her with resentment.

"I'm sorry," she said quickly. "It's not my business. I know that. Only, she loves you and it's such a waste of two lives!"

Jim rose, swept some papers together and said, curtly:

"I can't discuss it, Miss Sarat."

"Very well." She took her cue. "I'll go. But Jim — get out, make a new life — and marry Fran." She went to the door and opened it.

"You talk," his voice followed her, sharp and angry, "as though everything were so easy! What you don't realise, because you can't understand, is that sometimes the past lives on in the present and nothing you can do can rub it out!"

She turned, with her hand on the door handle.

"What past?"

His face became like a dark mask; even his anger was expunged from his features. "I have nothing more to say, Miss Sarat."

She said, quietly: "I'm sorry, Jim. But good luck if I don't see you again."

He came without a word to the front door, opened it and closed it behind her. She went along the narrow path, back past the rhododendron hedge, and paused to look back. He was standing in the lighted window watching her, immovable as a figure carved in dark wood.

Quickly Leonie went through the hornbeam garden and across the lawn to the house. For the first time she wondered whether Fran's happiness would lie after all with this man whom none of them really knew.

Lights showed in various rooms; Julian was nowhere about and as she closed the heavy front door she stood for a moment with her back to it. The hall lights had been left on for the last comer to turn out; the doors to the right and left of her were closed and there was no sound. Only, her eyes were drawn to the green baize door that led to the kitchen. It was swinging very gently as though someone had recently gone through. Someone wanting a glass of milk, a cool drink, some tea? She could do with something herself, yet, for the life of her, she couldn't go down that passage and through that door. . . .

After breakfast the following morning, Leonie went to her grandmother's room. Old Venetia was sitting up in bed wrapped in a shawl of white Chinese silk with yellow dragons embroidered on it. Above this splendour, her face looked very old; her skin transparent, her hair thin and white, drawn back from a face that had once enchanted.

She had three newspapers on the bed and a

cup of coffee was cooling on her bedside table.

"Ah, Leonie! You look pale, child!"

"I didn't sleep very well."

"Then you must take one of my pills to-night. They're quite harmless and not in the least habit-forming. You need a good night's sleep before the opening of the play."

"I know, Grandmother. That's why I thought —"

"You thought what?" she was smiling, watching her and appraising her.

"That I would go to my London flat for a few nights, just till the end of the week. By then I'll have got into my part and I'll come back here."

"If you can't sleep well here, you most certainly won't in London!"

"Oh, but my flat is very quiet."

"What disturbs you here?"

(Ghosts, Grandmother . . . ghosts . . . *and love*. . . .)

She said aloud, "I want to be on my own, just for a few days."

It sounded weak and she knew it.

"I'll come back," she rushed on.

"Of course you will. You won't play Fran's trick. I want you here, Leonie — at least for the rest of the month. It's good having you. There's no one as close to me as you — I'm proud of you and you're good for Julian, too! Perhaps," she plucked at the silken shawl, "perhaps in the end you'll come and live with us here for good."

Somewhere a clock chimed. Leonie said, grateful for the reminder:

"I'm afraid I must go now. But I'll be back probably at the end of the week."

"We shall be meeting on the second night of the play. You've got the seats, haven't you? And afterwards, there's my supper-party at the Savoy."

Leonie bent and kissed her. "I only hope you won't be disappointed in my performance."

"I shan't be." She settled back among her pillows. "There's a ticket for Fran, too, but she obviously won't be there! You still don't know where she is?"

"No —" she prayed her grandmother would let the matter drop. She did.

"Send Boadicea to me, Leonie, will you?" It was dismissal.

The sense of relief that she was leaving Heron House even for a few days made Leonie's packing of her small case almost a light-hearted thing.

XIV

That evening it was good to relax in her flat after an exacting dress rehearsal: good not to feel that she had to be on guard all the time; careful of what she said, listening for nuances and meanings in other people's words. Good to be alone! Just to sit there with her after-supper coffee and a newspaper crossword and the music from a Beethoven sonata playing over the radio filling the long, low room with lovely sound.

When the telephone bell rang, Leonie rose, half-crossed the room and then waited, hoping it would stop ringing before she reached it. She wanted no contact with anyone to-night. But it went on ringing and she lifted the receiver.

"Leonie?"

"Fran! For heaven's sake! Where are you? What in the world made you walk out like that?"

"I should have thought you'd know! Grandmother wanted to get rid of Jim —"

"I know that much!"

"And we quarrelled, and you know that, too!" she was speaking hurriedly, like someone wanting to get the whole explanation over. Then her voice changed, became less defiant, more intensive. "I'm glad I had that as an excuse for leaving Heron House because I see now, it was the only way out."

"The only way out of — what?"

"Well, I mean he wouldn't find it easy to get another place where he had a cottage. He knew he could have Gay and Chris looked after in his sister's house until he came home from work, but he wouldn't have felt that was making a home for them. So now, the only way out for him is to marry again."

"Marry you?"

"Yes. Even pig-headed Jim realises it's better to have a wife the children like than some stranger he isn't sure they'd take to. I've even said I'll give up the allowance my father makes me, if that'll please him. But I intend to use some of my aunt's legacy to buy us a house whether he likes it or not."

"Oh Fran, I'm so glad! You must be very happy about it all."

"Yes — yes, of course, I am." But the overlay of brightness in her tone made it only half a truth. Fran wasn't as happy about it all as she should have been.

"Something's still the matter, isn't it?"

"Pre-marriage nerves!" she laughed.

Leonie remained silent. Fran understood that silence only too well! She flared up.

"What do you think's the matter then? For heaven's sake, ever since you came to Richmond you started sensing atmospheres that weren't there. Now you're doing it with me! I'm marrying Jim and I love him and there's nothing more to it! Heron House is behind us; nothing's ever going to haunt me again!" she broke off with a small, audible gasp.

"Why do you attack me and then in the same breath admit that something haunted you, too?" For a long moment she thought Fran had left the telephone off its hook. She thought she had pushed her questions too far. Then Fran's voice came again.

"I'm sorry, Leonie, I suppose I resent the fact that you were honest enough to admit the atmosphere there and I wasn't. And now it's all over, we're free of it and I'll never go back!"

"You haven't told me where you are."

"I've found a furnished flat in a house overlooking Kew Gardens. Jim will join me here. It's only temporary until we can find a house with a garden for the children."

"Look, Fran, why not let us meet? I'm

staying in town for the next few days. Come along one evening and have supper with me."

"I – yes, perhaps I will –"

"Shall we fix a day?"

"No – I – I can't yet. You see, there's such a lot to do. We're being married in a few days' time, quietly with *no one* – no one we know there! I'm sorry, Leonie; you mustn't mind. We think it's best that way. And don't tell Grandmother. She's as capable as Marcus of ruining everything. Leonie – are you there?"

"Yes."

"Wish me luck!"

"Of course I do."

The line went dead.

Leonie replaced the receiver and guessed that Fran didn't want her at the wedding because she was a link with Heron House. She now had the man and the life she wanted, and yet she was on edge and still afraid. . . .

When the telephone rang ten minutes later, she thought it was Fran again. But it was Philip.

"I want to see you, Leonie. May I come round?"

"Oh Philip, yes! Or – perhaps, no! Perhaps it's better if –"

"It's 'Yes,'" he said firmly. "I'll be there in ten minutes."

Time to put on a dress, do her hair, put on some makeup. Time to tell herself this visit could be dangerous. Time to steady her heart. But not enough! Fran, Jim, Heron House were all forgotten. Philip had swept them away. When he came into the room, her blood raced, singing, through her body at the sight of him.

He said without preamble.

"I'm going to speak to Claire to-night — about us. I'll tell her about Marcus's part in it —"

"Philip, don't! Please don't say anything yet —"

He drew her down on to the settee and kept tight hold of one of her hands.

"I'll have to, Leonie. Last night Claire brought me a list of houses for sale. She wanted us to go down and see them because she said it would be a good idea to settle on one now so that she can spend the time until we can be married, decorating it as we want it. She has a dream of a kind of 'house beautiful' — the sort of place that gets photographed in the glossy magazines. *Now* do you understand why I've got to tell her immediately about us?"

She understood, of course, but she couldn't let him do it. For his own sake — and yet, how could she tell him what Claire had said; repeat the vicious words . . . ?

"Leonie, why are you so quiet? Look, darling, you must see that it would be impossible for me to go through the actual buying of a house for Claire and myself. I think it's a wild idea to want it now, but she argues that she has so little free time that it will take a long time to get the house as she wants it. I nearly told her about us last night and then I knew I had to speak to you, first."

She leaned back in her corner and felt her body shake with the hopelessness of it all. All the happiness he had dreamed about within her grasp — and she was unable to say with a free mind: "Yes, Philip, tell her —"

"I'm not married to Claire," Philip was saying. "Men and women make mistakes, engagements get broken —"

"But this tie is in a way stronger than an engagement — you must see that! And so much more difficult to break!"

She felt Philip's arm go round her. But she couldn't bear that! She got up and walked over to the mantelpiece, rested her elbow on it and hid her face in her hands. Her voice came, muffled and despairing.

"I can't marry you, Philip!"

"I won't believe it. I won't believe that what I heard was true!"

She turned and looked at him in surprise.

"What did you hear?"

"About you and Julian. I laughed when I was told. But perhaps I shouldn't have done. Perhaps –"

"Philip, what has been said – about Julian and me?"

"Sit down, you're trembling –"

"Tell me what was said!"

"Very well. Your grandmother told me that there was what was called 'a bond' between you two. She said that his marriage to Hilda was breaking up. Then, the other night –" he broke off, shaking his head.

"The other night," she cried, "Hilda saw Julian making a pass at me – I wasn't certain if she *had* seen or not. I was resisting, Philip. You should have known that!"

"I told you, I laughed when I was told. But when you said just now that you couldn't marry me, it all seemed to fit into place and become true!"

"So Hilda had to go and tell you –"

"No, Claire did. She was in the garden that night and she saw –"

"So it was Claire – it's always Claire, isn't it, watching –" she covered her face with her hands, "I'm sorry, Philip –"

"If Julian means nothing to you, why have you changed your mind about marrying me?"

"Claire has changed it."

"Because of what? Pity? Compassion? But she'll be all right after the operation – she'll be like any other girl, able to walk and dance. And she's young – there'll be other men –"

"I'm not thinking of that!" she met his eyes desperately. "But have you stopped to consider how Claire might react if you – if you give her up?"

"She'll be terribly upset. But I don't pride myself on being such a catch that she'll be broken-hearted. She's intelligent, too. In time she'll realise that no marriage can be based on the cowardice of one, and that's the way it would be if I went through with it. Cowardice on my part."

Leonie said, slowly. "Hell – hath – no – fury – like – a – woman – scorned –"

"That old adage! But that's positively medieval! In these days –"

"Men and women are fundamentally the same, Philip, whatever the day and age. The same love that – that can turn to hate!"

"Well, I'd deserve that!"

"But not in the form you might receive it."

"What do you mean?"

She shook her head dumbly. He began walking up and down the room.

"I've thought about it all until I can't think

any more. I've asked myself: What does a man do in these circumstances? Does he marry the girl knowing that all he'll ever feel is affection fanned by compassion and the hope that an old wound might be healed by caring for someone else? Well, Leonie, is that a sufficient basis for living a life of passionate lies?" He came and stood in front of her, waiting. "What would a man do? What would *you* do?"

"I'd tell —"

Philip put his arms out and caught her to him. "And so must I! My darling — Leonie — oh Leonie —" his lips were hard and hurting, "*This* is truth! This!" He leaned away from her, put a hand round her chin and raised her face. "And you *still* try to forbid me to talk to Claire?"

There was honesty and integrity in his face, in his grey eyes; there was also a sensitiveness, a capacity for being hurt. And how he would be hurt! She broke away from him and walked to the window, staring out at the golden light that suffused the trees of the little square.

Tell him what Claire told you! Go on, tell him!

"There's something I must say to you, Philip." She spoke with her back to him, her eyes on a little black poodle dancing over the grass.

Philip put his arms round her and drew her back against him. She felt his face against her hair.

"Tell me."

It was easier telling him like that, unable to see him. She left nothing out; Claire had said: "I could ruin Philip." "If, when I am free of Johnnie, he lets me down . . . . I'll do so much damage to his career. . . ." "I'm not a lawyer's daughter for nothing. I know ways in which I can harm Philip."

After the first few sentences, it became easier to tell — like a nightmare dragged out of you. . . .

She felt Philip's arms tighten across her breast with some emotion. Anger? Fear? She didn't dare turn round to find out. And then, when she had finished, he dropped his arms from her. There was utter silence in the room. *If only Philip would speak! If only I dare turn round and look at him and see on his face, my answer!* Can he go through with it? Can he now still say. "I will marry you, Leonie"? Or is too much at stake.

The waiting seemed endless, and then from somewhere far across the room, she heard him ask:

"Would it surprise you to know that *I* am not surprised?"

She swung round.

He was standing by the table, lighting a cigarette and his hands were quite steady.

"In my profession, I have to understand a little about people, Leonie. I have been Claire's constant companion for about a year, but I won't analyse her character to you except to say that, among all the things I had to consider, was the possibility that she might do just what you have said she threatens. The answer to it all rests with you, Leonie, not me."

"But my career wouldn't be hurt. Yours would —"

"Perhaps! Claire, you know, was left a lot of money by an aunt. She can afford to fight a long, bitter battle. How I would come out of it is quite an unknown factor. Such actions are tricky. I know. I'm not a lawyer for nothing. You see, once she's free of Johnnie, she can say we're engaged. She has proof enough that I was waiting to marry her."

The silence beat again about the low room. Every evening at this time, people came past the house on their way to evensong at the little church at the corner of the Square. It reminded Leonie of the time. She put her hands up, pushing back her hair.

"I've got to go, Philip. Some of the cast are meeting to-night to go through a last-minute change in one of the scenes."

"I'll take you where you want to go. But first
—" he put his hands on her arms and drew her
near to him. "Will you marry me, Leonie?"

"Yes." Her eyes were closed and she felt him
kiss her. "But please, Philip, please face the
fact that Claire can damage you!"

"Then we'll go and beachcomb in the South
Sea Islands and you can wear a grass skirt!
Now run along."

They were very quiet in the car on their way
to Juliet Pope's enormous flat in Covent
Garden. When he set her down in the deserted
back street, he said:

"This is my responsibility, Leonie, not
yours! Just let everything slide and remember
one thing. I love you." Then he gave her a
little salute and drove away.

But she couldn't let it slide, couldn't just pass
it over for him to cope with. She saw the tense,
nerve-racking days that Claire would force
upon him; the appearance in court, not on
someone else's tricky case, but his own. She
saw Claire playing her gentle, appealing part;
the accusations at connivance, the bribery of
Johnnie, the jury stung to pity. . . .

Whether Philip saw Claire that night or not,
Leonie had no idea. She heard nothing from
him the next day.

The Last Enchantment opened to a flourish of publicity since that veteran actress, Juliet Pope, was appearing in it. Temperaments had flown at the dress rehearsal and nothing was going right which, according to superstition, means that everything would be fine on the opening night!

It was now three days since she had seen Philip and he had made no attempt to contact her. She had to trust him — she *did* trust him because she knew him so well. Or did she? If a man's profession, something he had trained and worked hard for, was in jeopardy, could one be certain which way he would move in a crisis? But Philip's career couldn't possibly be irrevocably harmed by the case Claire might bring! He wasn't a criminal, and the law was just. . . . "I'm not a lawyer's daughter for nothing, I know ways in which I can harm Philip." Leonie found herself suddenly passionately hating and fearing the law. . . .

Desperately she clung to her faith in Philip's love for her. He had said they'd see this through together and they would. But why didn't he contact her? There was only one answer. As yet he hadn't found the courage to speak to Claire.

The play opened and from the very beginning the packed audience settled down to enjoy themselves. When the performance was over the applause was enthusiastic; there were endless curtain calls, shouts of "Bravo" for Juliet Pope. When Leonie stood alone and heard a spattering of those "Bravos" especially for herself she experienced that quiver of joy deep down in her that all the effort, all the fight she had had for a place in the theatre was worth while.

Back in her dressing-room there were more flowers arriving for her. And among them yellow roses. The tiny envelope tucked among the blooms had her name on it in Philip's handwriting. With a singing joy, she tore the envelope open. She read the words and then, quite quietly found that she was crying. The note just said:

"All kind wishes. Philip."

It was as though, behind those brief and formal words, she saw others engraved in fire. *"All over! I haven't the courage. Philip."*

She sat at her dressing-table and tears streamed down her face.

"It's just nerves, love!" said the cockney dresser. "Go on, you cry!" She shook out the flame-coloured dress Leonie wore in the last act. "What shall I do with those lovely flowers? There ain't much more room —"

Leonie waved them aside. She couldn't speak.

That night, at the party, she sat like a ghost. The rest of the cast were thrilled and happy. They were sufficiently experienced to smell success. They ate and drank and laughed and nobody noticed that Leonie was barely one of them.

XV

After the second night's performance, Venetia walked into Leonie's dressing-room and swept her into her arms, congratulating her on her performance. Other people entered the room, were introduced to Venetia and conversation danced around Leonie.

When the four of them reached their table at the Savoy there was a bowl of odontoglossum orchids on the table with a note for Venetia from Philip.

She leaned forward and touched them with pleasure.

"He must have heard his father say that I always had them on my table when I dined here! And he remembered!" she turned to Leonie. "He can't join our supper-party, by the way! Claire isn't well and he rang up just as we were leaving to say that he would be bringing her back from her office to Heron House."

Leonie made no comment. So Philip couldn't face her! Sometimes, when hope could sink no further, speech was impossible. . . .

"Poor little Claire," Hilda was saying, sentimentally. "It's probably that leg of hers hurting —"

"It's nothing of the kind," Venetia interrupted. "She thinks she's got a cold. Where's the wine waiter? Where's the menu?" She swung round and found both patiently at her elbow. "Ah!" she appraised the young man who set the enormous menu before her. "You're too young to remember me. I used to come here many years ago. We had great parties in those days and we dressed up in fine clothes and jewels. You'll never see that kind of lavishness now. It's gone — for ever."

The young waiter made some polite remarks and supper was ordered. Old Venetia was gay and willed them to be gay with her. But while Julian did his best, Hilda was most uneasy. She would not look directly at Leonie and when they drank a little toast to her success, Hilda's eyes looked down into her wine glass and her lips barely formed the words.

Venetia began to talk about her old days on the stage. Leonie had never seen her so animated, as though she were in her element here in one of the familiar restaurants of her greatness.

Leonie was a fascinated listener.

After a particularly amusing story of Venetia

241

as a very young girl awed by her first stage appearance with the great Sarah Bernhardt, she glanced at Hilda and Julian. With almost a shock she saw that neither of them was making much more than a polite pretence at listening.

Presently, with her characteristic quick change of conversation, old Venetia glanced at the orchids on the table and said:

"I wonder if my new gardener, who, by the way, has the outlandish name of Archibald Angry, can grow orchids. I think I must talk to him about them. You know," she addressed Leonie, "Fran's outburst was quite ridiculous! I am quite certain that Jim's glad to leave — a comparatively small garden can't really interest an ambitious man. The new man, Angry, is older — he looks rather like a surprised gnome, but he has excellent references. He has a wife who will help Boadicea in the house. So it is all working out very well! Jim is storing his furniture and moving into some furnished flat he has found near Kew Gardens." She glanced at Leonie. "So, if you see Fran, you can tell her that her temper was pointless."

Leonie lifted her glass and made a pretence at savouring the excellent wine Venetia had ordered.

"*Have* you seen Fran yet?" Venetia asked.

Leonie gave her an honest "No."

"Well, we really can't waste our energies wondering what is happening to her. I don't expect a guest to walk out on me, even a granddaughter. Her parents seem to have omitted to teach her good manners! Julian, some more wine, please."

The conversation changed. But Leonie knew that Fran was not naturally ill-mannered, nor was she temperamental by nature. She was frightened because she wasn't certain whether the man she loved had been involved in a murder, and she had no previous experience to draw on which could help her tackle her situation.

She could ask Jim but how would she know whether to believe him if he denied it? It was Leonie's guess that she did not dare to try to find out!

While they were having coffee, the orchestra began to play a medley of Schubert music.

Venetia sat up; her eyes sparkled.

"That's especially for me! See, they're looking my way and smiling. Someone remembers me! Someone who knew my favourite music! My beloved Schubert!" She sat up very straight, eyes watching the players, humming softly under her breath. As the music came to a close two people paused by their table.

"You see?" asked a man's voice. "I have never forgotten your likes, Venetia!"

She looked up. "Brad Levanthon!" she cried.

"That's right. All the way from Virginia."

"And Marnie!" Venetia exclaimed and smiled at the little woman with the blonde hair and the pastel mink stole who stood by his side. "I haven't seen either of you in years!"

"Two," he reminded her. He was tall and very broad, grey-haired and his spectacles were as large as owl's eyes.

Venetia considered his correction. Animation sparkled in her eyes.

"Of course, I remember now! We met at the reception given for Juliet Pope in New York. We've been to see her to-night in the new play at the Shelton. My granddaughter," she indicated Leonie, "is also appearing in it."

Introductions were made. Brad had once been a distinguished actor on Broadway.

"We've been touring Europe," he explained. "We do it every year and we never get tired of the same old places — you know, Paris and Rome, Venice and London. Come to that," he added, "*you* didn't see *me*, but I saw you a year ago at the air car-ferry. We'd just come over from the Riviera and your car was released just before ours."

Venetia's face was a blank.

244

"So I have a double! I don't know whether to be flattered or not!"

"But I'm sure it was you. I recognised Julian, too! It was April of last year —"

"You are mistaken," Venetia spoke lightly. "Quite mistaken! We came over here only about three months ago. My husband died some two years ago and I have been restless to return to England."

"Oh, but —" and then Brad Levanthon stopped, looked puzzled, and concerned: "Well, my sight isn't as good as it was. Maybe you've both got doubles." He looked at Hilda. "All three of you have, I guess!"

Leonie heard Hilda's sharp intake of breath. She was sitting up straight in her chair and her face was very red. Her eyes were resting on the stranger as though he were a demon from the dark regions. She was terrified.

Julian was lighting a cigarette. His hands were quite steady, but a small muscle at the side of his mouth twitched.

When the American couple had moved away with copious handshakes, Venetia became herself again and seemed amused by the whole affair.

"I suppose I should have invited them to Heron House. How foolish of me not to have thought of it. Never mind, another year, if we ever meet again!"

Julian drew hard on his cigarette, saying nothing. Hilda remained, hands on her lap twisting and untwisting, staring at Venetia.

"Julian," said the old lady suddenly, "I would like a brandy."

"Of course." He called the waiter. Hilda said she would have one too. Leonie refused. But, sitting there watching them, one thought struck across the efforts at conversation. *A year ago, on an April evening, Marcus had been killed. . . .*

They left the Savoy very soon after the meeting with the Americans. Julian drove Venetia's car, taking Leonie home first.

Her grandmother had been silent for some time, sitting back in a corner of the car, her face shadowed. Then, as they turned into the square where Leonie lived, old Venetia drew a little sobbing breath. Her head fell on to her chest and her hand was pressed under her sables, against her heart.

"Julian, Grandmother's ill!"

He drew into the kerb and stopped the car. Then he got out and came and opened the door.

"Her bag," he groped on the floor for it and got out a little phial, unscrewing the top and shaking two tablets into her hand.

"Here, Venetia, take these."

Leonie had her arm around her grandmother and was turning to raise her head. Hilda had turned and was half-kneeling on the front seat, her hands gripping the back of it, saying: "Oh! Oh Julian, be quick!" like a frightened child.

But his fingers fumbled as he tried to get her to swallow the tablet and he dropped one of them on to the floor of the car.

"Here, let me." Leonie snatched the second tablet from him and gave it to Venetia. Julian shook another from the bottle and this one was more difficult to swallow without water. But Venetia managed it and she lay for a few minutes, panting, but she no longer fought for breath. Then she gave a sigh.

"I'll be all right – now –"

Leonie looked at Julian and he nodded.

"She's had these turns before. It's a mild form of angina. After all, at her age –"

"Don't discuss me as though I weren't here," she panted testily. She was most certainly better.

Leonie's arm was still round her and she felt the light weight of the body against her. Julian replaced the phial and got back into the driver's seat.

"We'll just wait here quietly for a few minutes," he said.

They sat in silence, Hilda continually turning round to look at Venetia, whose eyes were closed. Leonie sat with her arm about her grandmother and studied the sleek fair head of Julian and was puzzled by him. She had watched him working at his little theatre, noticing the beautiful precision of his fingers – and yet he could not give a sick woman tablets without fumbling, without wasting precious moments that could have cost a life. . . .

Venetia stirred, sat up and said:

"I'm quite all right now. It must have been the excitement – children and old people get like that, you now. Children get sick; old people have heart attacks!" She laid a hand on Leonie's arm. "Come back with us to Richmond to-night; don't stay away –"

"But Grandmother –"

"You've got through the first two performances of the play; you're perfectly safe in your part now so there's no excuse for not coming back with us."

"I'd like to have a few more days –"

"And I, my child, would like to see as much of you as I can – while I can! I'm over eighty and one day there won't be any pills that can help me!"

It was the first time Leonie had known

Venetia to play on sympathy and it defeated her.

"I'll come back, Grandmother," she said gently. "But I must first go to my flat and fetch my things."

"Of course."

When they were outside the house, Venetia said: "Go along up and pack. Julian, go with Leonie and bring her case down for her."

"No, don't bother. It won't be heavy!"

But Julian was already out of the car.

"Can he bring you down a little brandy, Grandmother?"

"Why, yes, I think I'd like some. But don't give me too much." She sat hunched in her sables with Philip's orchids in her lap. "Run along. Run along. I want to get back home."

Upstairs in the empty flat, Leonie went first to the drink cupboard and poured out the brandy into a glass. Julian took it from her.

"I'll wait for you."

"No don't. I shall be a few minutes. Take that down to Grandmother. By the way, does she really get these attacks often?"

"No. They usually come on when she's over-excited."

"And you have to give her the tablets? I mean, she can't get them for herself?"

"Sometimes, if she feels the attack coming

on, she can get them for herself."

And at other times she was dependent for her very life on the speed with which someone gave her the nitroglycerine tablets. And one day, if Julian fumbled as he had done to-night, it would be too late and she would die. . . .

Leonie steadied her thoughts. Julian, standing there smiling at her, was no sinister figure. She watched him turn and go out of the room with the brandy glass, and across her memory came the old Arab proverb. "There is a dark, secret side to every bright, open face."

She closed the cupboard door firmly and went into her bedroom and pushed a few things back into her case. Then she turned out the lights, closed her door and went downstairs to the car.

They were all very quiet during the drive to Richmond, and more than once during the journey the little lurking suspicion stole back to trouble her. When Venetia died, Julian would be rich. When Venetia died, Hilda would give him his freedom and sit back happily with her fat alimony. . . .

'There is a dark, secret side . . .' *Stop it! Stop it!* she told herself. If there were only someone she could talk to. Philip, for instance. Philip – her heart ached with her loneliness for him. . . .

When they arrived at the house, Leonie suggested that they should make up a bed for Venetia in one of the ground-floor rooms.

"While I can climb to my bedroom, I will," she retorted. "I've taken the trouble to make it beautiful and I wish to lie there. Leonie. Hilda. Help me upstairs, please. I don't want to break my neck."

They were nearly at the top when someone came from the back of the house. Claire, with a limping run, stood at the bottom of the stairs, looking up at them.

"Oh, what's happened?"

Old Venetia paused and glanced down at her.

"Nothing, Claire, except that I had a little pain and I'm going to bed now. What about you, by the way; I hear you've got a cold?"

"I thought I had, but it was probably just overtiredness. I've been working awfully hard on that house, but Philip has been spoiling me. He left about an hour ago."

While she spoke, she put up her hand to her hair. On the little finger the diamond and aquamarine ring Philip had given her sparkled and danced.

"The best thing you can do is to go to bed," old Venetia advised. "It's very late."

"I know, but Philip and I have been listening to some music. It was all so restful that I'm no longer tired and I wanted to stay until you came home."

So, in spite of all that he had said, Philip had not spoken to Claire. In spite of all his brave words, his courage was not equal to the strength of his heart!

Boadicea was sent for to help Venetia undress. The rest of them dispersed, Hilda still with that look of frozen fear in her eyes, shivering under her lovely fur wrap.

After unpacking her few things, Leonie went downstairs to the drawing-room. It was empty, and in the silence the little gilded Louis Quinze clock ticked softly. Leonie thought with longing of her own comfortable living-room and went to the window, too restless to admit her tiredness.

Through the trees she could see that there was a light in the cottage. But Jim had gone! Or had he? Had something happened at the last minute to upset all Fran's plans?

Whatever had happened, it was not for her to probe and interfere. Yet she found herself bent on doing just that! She was out of the house almost before she realised it, walking along the paths, lit faintly by moonlight; through the hornbeam garden where the lupins were like the little spears of a pygmy army.

The front door of the cottage was open and

one light was on in the sitting-room. But it was Claire, not Jim, standing at a table. Her head was bent over a small book and her attention was so caught that she did not even hear the sound of footsteps on the gravel path.

Leonie went through the front door and stood on the threshold of the living-room.

"Hallo, Claire."

The girl started and swung round.

"For heaven's sake. How you creep around, Leonie!"

"As it happens, my spindly heels make rather a lot of noise. You were very engrossed." She glanced at the book in Claire's hands.

"I came out for a breath of air. I just happened to pass the cottage and saw that there was a pile of stuff not cleared away. Idle curiosity got the better of me!"

Leonie glanced at the assortment on the table. Old toys and picture books, piles of postcards and odds and ends from a children's play-cupboard. She remembered Venetia had said that Jim was going to fetch them and take them to a children's hospital.

In Claire's hand was a small, brightly-coloured book. She had it open at a page and Leonie saw childish handwriting.

"It's an old diary of Gay's," Claire explained, and indicated the coloured pictures at the tops

253

of the pages. "Pretty, isn't it? That is —" she paused significantly, "until you read a certain content." Eyebrows raised, she looked at Leonie. "Want to see?"

"No. Gay's diary is her own affair."

"Evidently she didn't think it important enough to keep! It's last year's. She's probably forgotten all about it."

"I should imagine it got caught up in that pile of stuff by mistake. Jim wouldn't want to send *that* to a children's home. We'd better destroy it."

"Oh, no!" Claire held on to it firmly. "Finding's keepings!" she said, "and this may be very useful if people here start to be inquisitive!"

"How do you mean?" Leonie heard her own voice as frozen as an enemy's — but then Claire was her enemy and she hated having to face her, look at her, talk to her.

"Shall I read you something I've just seen in Gay's diary?"

"Give it to me!"

"I think you'd better listen. It's rather incriminating. It's what the police would describe as 'throwing a new light' on what happened that — er — fatal night!" She bent her dark head. "Don't they teach children to spell any more? But never mind. It's what she writes that matters! Listen to this:"

"It's a child's private possession." Leonie began to walk quickly towards the door.

Claire ignored her. "The date is in April last year and Gay writes: 'Daddy was angry to-day. I wanted him to mend my china dog because it got broke. But he was in the kitchen, shouting that nobody must let him meet Mr. Sarat that day because if he did he'd kill him! and Miss Fran's voice said, *Don't*, and Daddy said something to her and then I was frightened and ran away.'"

Leonie stood rooted in the doorway. Claire raised her head and looked at her.

"A child's written declaration could be damning, couldn't it, Leonie, if people started to probe further into Marcus's death?"

"Give me that diary. It's not yours to read!"

"Nor yours! Don't be silly! It proves, doesn't it, that Jim was furiously angry about something and that Fran was scared? After all, Jim was a commando towards the end of the war, he —"

Leonie's hand shot out, moved with a powerful involuntary impulse, and snatched the book from Claire.

"I don't think it matters much!" Claire said very softly, "whether you destroy it or not, now! You see, Gay is old enough to remember what happened so that any clever detective would get it out of her — *if* I were ever to mention the diary to the police. I'd have to say, too, wouldn't I, that you destroyed the book? Gay would admit, under their gentle questioning, that she had kept a diary and you wouldn't come out of the whole affair very well, Leonie!"

"You can't mean that you're going to the police."

"No! No, I don't think I shall. Not, that is, unless things become difficult for me. You know, dear, what I mean, don't you?" The childlike quality of her voice made her menacing words a horrible reality.

With the diary in her hands Leonie turned and walked out of the room. She went quickly across the garden and into the house by the back entrance. In the kitchen she turned on the light and looked at the little book. She found the page that had at the top of it a charming drawing of daisies and a young fawn. She saw the words, exactly as Claire had read them. Gay had heard her father's threat; she had heard Fran's voice protesting. And suddenly Leonie knew why Fran was afraid. She was not certain, she would never be certain, that Jim had not killed Marcus! She loved him; she knew that if in a terrible moment he had done this thing, it was for her sake. But she faced the fact that he could be violent and she was prepared to marry him — perhaps already had married him — because she loved him. With her, if Jim had accidentally killed Marcus, his secret would be safe because, as his wife, she would be unable by law to give evidence against him. . . .

She went into the stone passage-way and threw the diary into the furnace.

The matter would never be closed because of Claire; because this was something else she would hold over the head of Fran or Jim or Leonie if it suited her. A man's life was perhaps in those small, pointed hands that could create such beauty while the mind that impelled their every movement held such malevolence.

XVI

The house remained in its aura of uneasiness for the next two days. Leonie's evenings were now spent at the theatre, and she managed to find reasons for remaining in town for most of the day, so that she saw little of Heron House except as a place to sleep.

On the following Sunday she went to see some friends in the country and returned about ten o'clock.

The house seemed deserted, the living-room was empty. The day had been cloudy and faintly damp and when night fell there was a chill in the air. Leonie crossed the great living-room and switched on the electric heater.

As she straightened, she saw, lying on the mantelpiece, the great key to the music-room. Venetia must have used and forgotten to put it back in her bag. She picked it up, recalling how as a little girl its intricate brass-work had intrigued her.

And then she remembered that she had never had a chance to secure the window of the alcove. Probably nobody had noticed that it wasn't locked, but for security's sake, it should be done.

With the key in her hand, she went to the door of the room and listened. Hilda and Julian had probably gone to their bedroom; Claire was nowhere around; Boadicea was with Venetia. This, then, was the perfect moment to slip in and fasten the window.

She went quickly downstairs and along the passage. The key slid smoothly into place, the lock turned and she was inside. She switched on the light and, without pausing, went into the alcove and fastened the window.

She was turning away when her gaze fell on the great pile of press-cutting books she had seen only a few days ago when she had released Claire. She went over and opened the top one, flicking the pages. They were pasted with theatrical photographs, old programmes, articles, eulogies – all about Venetia. How beautiful she had been with her arresting eyes and her tempestuous mouth and that lovely, cleancut chin! How magnificently she had played the great roles created by Ibsen and Pirandello, by Shaw and Maugham! These books were a record of a fantastic high-powered publicity, volume after volume of them from Venetia Sarat's earliest theatre days almost up to the present. In one half-filled volume which was the last of them, were snapshots of the house in New Orleans, of Venetia with her husband, Venetia with her horses and her great beach house near the Florida everglades; of Julian and a very few of Hilda, stuck in the corners as a concession, no doubt, to her status as Julian's wife. In the photographs of the interior of her home Leonie recognized some of the furniture here at Heron House. There were photographs of her small, exotic garden, her dogs and even of her great, ancient car. It was, by present-day standards, almost a caricature of a car. Leonie looked at it with interest. It was like a high, elegant box on wheels with the unmistakable design of bonnet used by an exclusive car manufacturer. It belonged to an earlier age and was so high-slung that you could almost get into it standing up! Parked outside the New Orleans house, it reached nearly to the top of the wall.

Almost as high as the wall running along the back of Heron House. . . .

Leonie's words, her words to the detective-inspector who had interrogated her . . . "I saw the top of a car over the wall. . . ."

But there were no such high-slung cars these days, they had all said. Or perhaps, just one here and there, owned by eccentrics or jokers or octogenarians who clung to the past. . . .

Suddenly Leonie laid the press-cutting book flat; she took hold of the snapshot of the car standing outside the New Orleans house and carefully peeled it from the page. It came away easily enough as though its pasting had been very light. Like a conspirator, her heart thudding with a slow, terrifying, dawning knowledge, she closed the book, replaced it where she had found it at the bottom of the pile and stole from the room.

With the key safely back on the mantelpeice in the drawing-room and the snapshot tucked in her notecase, Leonie went to bed.

She lay there, trying to put the pieces of the jigsaw together and scarcely daring to believe the picture which was emerging. Brad Levanthon had said that very night that he had seen Venetia and Julian and Hilda at the air ferry a year ago. Venetia had denied it; but there had been terror on Hilda's face and had it been the shock of that recognition which had brought on her grandmother's heart attack? Venetia Sarat had been seen in England at the time of Marcus's death – and she had once owned just the kind of ancient, high-slung car that could have been seen over a garden wall. . . .

It was merely coincidence. . . . Or was it?

Hilda had said: "I know who killed Marcus," before fear made her retract her statement. Who had killed him? Had Venetia with Julian and Hilda, been harmlessly visiting Marcus on their tour of Europe, and seen something that placed them all in danger if they had ever dared to admit they had been here? But if that were so, why had Venetia come here to live? Because she was a woman without fear? Or because she had seen nothing and only Hilda and Julian knew?

I must show that snapshot to Philip. I must tell him, Leonie thought. And then remembered that she couldn't. Philip had been avoiding her so carefully since that evening when she had told him of Claire's threats, that it seemed unlikely that she would ever see him alone again.

Moonlight cast a milky glow over the ceiling; dimly she heard a car revving up the hill. This was no dark dream, it was a reality — and one that she must face. Philip had kissed her and said he loved her . . . and then gone out of her life. . . .

For two days Leonie lived in the house on Richmond Hill with a sense of her own unreality. She walked, moved, talked and even sometimes, laughed, in a dream. Only when she was on the stage at the Shelton Theatre did her will-power take over and carry her through her performance. At the house, nothing happened, nothing was said, nothing done that heightened or deepened the mystery. Claire came and went, but Leonie scarcely saw her because in the evenings she was at the theatre and when she came home she went straight to bed.

On Sunday Leonie again went into the country to see some friends. When she returned, she told the driver to take her to the back entrance in the lower road. She wanted to look at that wall, to see how the taxi top measured against it.

When she got out and paid the driver she saw that the modern cab was considerably below the height of the wall – and it told her nothing.

She went through the gate, pausing for a moment to get accustomed to the darkness which the bushes threw across her path.

At first she thought it was very quiet, and then she heard a sound. Someone was whistling, just a few bars over and over again. It was a nervous sound, as though the tune had such a grip on the whistler that he could not stop. As though, she thought, he were trying to exorcise a ghost theme haunting his mind.

A few bars! But strangely, terrifyingly

familiar! A tune only two or three people knew. *The theme of Marcus's proposed piano concerto played over to himself, but never put to paper. . . .*

Leonie stood rooted in the shadows. That haunted sound! That rushed, desperate whistle. . . .

She turned towards the sound and saw a light in the summer-house. Julian was there. Julian! But how could he know the theme music unless he had been there when Marcus was playing it?

And suddenly it all fitted into place.

The whistling stopped abruptly and Leonie realised that she must have made a sound. She moved cautiously along the path. Julian was at his bench, his head turned towards the door of the summer-house, watching for her.

"Hallo, Leonie."

"What was that you were whistling as I came by?"

"I can't remember. Something milling round in my mind," he answered lightly.

He can't hurt me, she thought. He likes me too much! He'd break down and confide, but he would never dare harm me. People are quite near . . . in the house. . . .

She said quietly, trying not to shock him:

"The week-end before Marcus died, I came

here, Julian and I found him in a state of great excitement. He had worked out the theme for his new concerto. He said it was still in his head and it wouldn't be put down on paper for a long time. That was the way he worked. He lived with a musical idea before he finally set it down on paper. But *you* knew it!"

Julian didn't seem to move, but the toy chair he was holding fell to the ground. From somewhere inside him came a queer, struggling laugh.

"Well! Well! What a coincidence, since I know nothing about Marcus's music! The tune must be in the air, and I picked it up," he tried to laugh. "Don't you think, since I'm so clever, I might do a turn in revue? You know: '*You* think of a tune, *I* whistle it!' " he was talking fast and his voice was pitched high.

Then, because Leonie said nothing – she had no previous memory to tell her what to do in such circumstances, her silence unnerved him.

"I don't know what you're thinking, but if it's what it seems, then – Leonie, for God's sake, you don't think *I* came here that evening when Marcus was killed and talked to him?"

"If you weren't here, how could you know that music?"

"A few bars! Look –" his mind was

265

obviously racing to find reasons. "Marcus played it over and over – you said so! Well then, the gardener could have heard it while he was working near the house – I could have picked it up from him. That's it! I remember now, I heard him humming it while he was in the vegetable garden."

"I've never in my life heard Jim hum a tune. He's a very silent person."

In the stark light of the studio-summer-house, Julian's eyes seemed abnormally bright. Leonie felt a curious fear, a kind of instinct that if she moved, if she began to run towards the house, she would be in danger. She must remain calm, remain here and see this thing through.

Julian was gaining confidence.

"Be sensible, Leonie! How could I know that tune – except by having heard someone else hum or whistle it? I was thousands of miles away when Marcus was thinking it out!"

"But these people we met to-night said they saw you –"

"You heard what Venetia said. We all have doubles."

"Three of them? That's a coincidence!"

Somewhere she heard a car start up. Philip's? But Philip wouldn't be here to-night, not when there was a risk of seeing Leonie. . . .

She was aware of a movement. Julian's hand shot out and she backed quickly, in alarm.

"Leonie," his fingers caught her arm. "You don't think *I* killed Marcus, do you?"

Some instinct for her own preservation made her say, "No. No, of course, I don't, Julian!"

"You really mean that?"

"Yes," she said and hoped desperately that he was convinced. "All I want to try and find out is if you were here that night Marcus was killed; if you heard or saw anything. Perhaps you did – and you're afraid to say."

She heard him give a long sigh, as though he had been holding his breath. There was no movement anywhere in the dark garden, no sign of lights in the house from this remote corner. She might have been in the wilderness alone with Julian – who knew too much!

"What could I see," he was asking her, "since I wasn't here? You're letting your imagination run wild, aren't you?"

She watched his hands. Sensitive, but strong; hands that had fumbled when trying to give old Venetia her tablets. . . . On purpose?

"What's the matter? What are you thinking?"

She was silent. Why did I start this? I must have been mad. If I could only get back to the house . . . if Julian would take his eyes off me, just for a moment. . . .

"You're trying to trick me," he said, "aren't you, Leonie? You're just waiting until I crack. As though I will! As though I have anything — to — to — crack — about —"

"I'm not trying to trick you. I just want to know things. How you knew that tune. Why Hilda is so frightened all the time. Why you are all denying that you were here last year when you were seen. So much evidence piling up, Julian — too much to be just coincidence! That's why I'm asking —"

"Stop it! Stop it!" he suddenly shouted. "I didn't kill Marcus!"

"I'm not even asking that. All I want to know is if you were here on that night. You see, Julian, I told the police about a car I'd noticed going along the lower road very slowly, as though it was just starting up. A very high-slung car, the sort we don't use nowadays. But Grandmother had one, didn't she? Were you touring Europe in it last year?"

"How do you know we had an old car?"

"There is a snapshot of it in one of the albums in the music-room. I happened to see it. It all adds up, Julian, to the fact that you were here —"

Three times he tried to speak, and couldn't. His face was dead white in the studio lights.

She was silent. If I could escape, she

thought, back to the house . . . to safety.

All right," he said. "All right, Leonie. You've worked it all out, haven't you? I *was* here. We had been touring Europe and Venentia wanted to see Marcus about this house. He wouldn't answer her letters and so at the end of our two weeks' tour of England, we came here on the evening before our return to the States. We came here — but I never talked to Marcus! There was someone — running away from the house as we arrived —"

"Who?"

He said: "I don't know," and his eyes slewed away from her.

But he did know — and so did Hilda. *I know who killed Marcus . . .* she had said.

"Julian —" Leonie began and then stopped.

His eyes, looking past her, held petrified fear.

Leonie wheeled round. Venetia stood there in the pool of light from the studio. She wore the green dress Leonie had seen when she first came to Heron House weeks ago, and she stood just as straight, just as quietly.

"We were talking" — Leonie began to break that awful silence — "about what happened —"

"On the might of Marcus's death. Yes, I heard you." Venetia's voice was strong and clear. "A little while ago I heard Julian shouting like a hysteric. So I came out to see what it was all about —"

"Leonie knows that we were here a year ago."

"Leonie *knows* nothing!" retorted old Venetia. "She only guesses. She is obsessed with a mystery she can't clear up and so she plays around with wild theories. And now she has got you playing them, too! I suggest you both grow up and stop this childish nonsense."

"Leonie wasn't guessing —"

Venetia rounded on Julian. "How stupid can you be? As though we're magicians and can be in two places at once!"

"Grandmother —" Leonie took charge. "When the police questioned me at the time, I said I saw a car that night going along the lower road and they said I must have been mistaken because modern cars were too low-slung to be seen over the back wall. But you toured Europe in that high car of yours — it was an old make — but I should think very luxurious.

"How do you know about my car?"

"I've seen a photograph of it."

"Where?"

"In one of those albums in the music-room."

In the momentary silence, old Venetia made a quick, slashing gesture with her hand.

"What are you?" Her voice was soft. "A little spy? Prying and questioning −"

"Tell her." Julian's voice rose. "Tell Leonie that I didn't kill Marcus!"

Venetia's sudden laughter was broken by Hilda's voice calling her. She was running up the path from the dark place outside the patch of light in which they stood.

"Fran is on the telephone for you. She wants to explain, she says, and say she's sorry she behaved as she did. Venetia −" Hilda's voice trailed off. She came to a sudden stop and stared, wide-eyed, at the small silent group. "Wh − what's − happened?"

Julian spoke.

"Leonie knows that we were here on the night Marcus was killed."

Hilda cried out. Her hand flew to her mouth. Behind her fingers her voice came muffled and aghast.

"Oh Julian! Oh dear God!"

"You know, don't you, Hilda, that I didn't kill Marcus?"

There was a dead silence.

"You *know* −" Julian repeated, his voice harsh. "Hilda, stop looking at me like that! Tell Leonie −"

Hilda began to whimper; it was a small, crushed hopeless little sound. Then she struggled for words.

"Tell the truth, Julian! Please, oh please, tell the truth! It'll be better in the end. It *was* in self-defence, wasn't it! Marcus attacked you —"

"What the devil are you talking about?"

"You and Marcus. It would be better —"

" 'Better?' " Venetia swung round on her. "Oh, you fool!"

Hilda ignored her. "It was an accident. You didn't mean to kill him, Julian?"

"But I *didn't!* I keep telling everyone I didn't kill him. For the love of heaven, someone believe me!" He looked desperately from one to the other.

Leonie heard Hilda gasp. Venetia struck the door with a hard, angry fist.

"You? You — kill?" She seemed to have grown taller, stronger. She dominated that black and gold scene at the studio door.

"Then who?" Leonie felt cold horror creep over her.

Venetia was watching her.

"Very well, Leonie, since you can't leave the past alone, we *did* come here, all three of us. I wanted to talk to Marcus; we came to the back gate so that he shouldn't see the car in the drive and pretend to be out. I intended to walk in on him — there was a lot I had to say to him! This was *my* house, Leonie. I was born here.

272

Marcus tricked me out of it when I was no longer here in England to keep an eye on my property. When we arrived that night, we heard someone running from the house. I know now that it was Claire. That is why she would never admit to knowing Marcus! Claire!" she paused. "Well, is it all clear to you now?"

"You mean – it was – Claire –"

"Who killed Marcus?" Old Venetia's eyes did not waver. "Your guess is as good as mine. Nothing can be proved now, but –"

"You wouldn't dare." Julian's voice was suddenly strong, whipping across Venetia's. "You wouldn't dare throw suspicion on Claire! We can only guess that it was she we heard running away that night from the house."

"Some guesses are good – and accurate!"

They were facing one another now. Venetia and her adopted son.

"Whether she was here or not isn't important," he said, "because Marcus was alive after she left. You know it – you spoke to him."

In the studio lights the old eyes were light gold, like an animal's.

"Well, so I spoke to him!" she said softly. "And what does that prove? Exactly nothing. Marcus was alone in the house, so no one – *no* one, my dear Julian – will ever know who killed him! Questions! Questions! That's all there'll ever be! *Did* Claire come back that night after we'd gone? And where were you, Julian, when Marcus was killed?"

Leonie saw their gaze hold; saw bitter antagonism.

"Stop! Oh stop all this!" Hilda cried. "What *is* it neither of you will say?"

No one took the slightest notice of her. Above them the trees began to rustle.

"Someone was here that night," Hilda rushed on, "and saw whoever it was who – who killed Marcus. Someone knows!"

"Claire –"

Leonie was not certain who said her name because suddenly something struck her. She cried:

"Jim was here – in spite of what was said in the witness box about him being at Kew, Jim was here and saw – saw – *whom?*"

"So that's who it was running away from the house! Marcus's gardener!" Hilda breathed with awe.

"But he didn't kill Marcus, did he?" Leonie heard her voice; heard her own ring of clear conviction. "You said – he was alive after – after someone was seen running away."

"The person we saw – was a woman!"

Julian's voice shook so much that the words were scarcely audible. But they had the ring of truth. A woman, not a man!

"I don't believe Jim was around at all!" Julian said. "The cottage was in darkness. I — saw. Jim must have been where he said — at Kew —" Words seemed to stick in his throat. He was so consumed with fear that, without realising it, Leonie reached out and touched him on the arm.

As though her contact was a switch, he responded immediately. Desperate strength seemed to flow back. He took a step forward.

"Tell her, Venetia. For God's sake tell them all. Don't let someone innocent be suspected. Jim didn't kill Marcus! Claire didn't! It was she we saw running away, and if she came back again to the house after we'd gone, then she found Marcus dead! That must be why she kept quiet — in case people thought she had killed him."

"No one will ever know," Venetia said in her clear, carrying voice. "No one will ever be able to prove anything now!"

"You're wrong. Venetia, you're quite wrong! Leonie can. She has evidence that —"

"You fool! Oh you fool!"

"But I'm not afraid. You can't harm me here — not with others around; not with me on my guard. It's too late, Venetia, too late to dismiss it all and say, 'What's done is done!' It's all *here* – Leonie knows so much – she's very near to knowing everything –"

At what moment Venetia started to run, Leonie had no idea. But she turned and saw her stumbling away blindly through the semi-darkness, panting, crying, mumbling to herself.

Hilda's voice broke in.

"Oh God! Julian – I thought it was you. I always –"

"Venetia was right," he said in a dead voice. "You should have known that even if I'd hated Marcus, I could never kill."

"And I was so afraid. Julian –" she stammered. "I daren't say anything to you – it was too awful even to – breathe about! You were my husband and – and –"

"You thought I killed Marcus. And you thought, I suppose, that if I guessed you knew, I'd stop at nothing to prevent you giving me away!" He looked at her with pity.

Leonie waited to hear no more. She was running after Venetia. Hilda cried after her:

"Leonie, the telephone; I forgot. Fran's hanging on –"

Perhaps she was, but it was the last thing that mattered to Leonie at that moment. She had reached the garden door to the music-room.

There was a light on and the old woman was by the wall safe, her hands agitated. She was talking to herself, rapidly and angrily.

"I – don't – remember." She twisted and fumbled at the knob. "I can't – remember –" and then her anger fell away from her and she began to whimper like a child. "The – combination –"

"I know it, Grandmother," Leonie said. "Let me," and reached up and manipulated the knob. The little steel door opened.

"There are two papers in there." Venetia was crouched in the chair beneath the water-colour that hid the safe. "Give – them – to me. They are tied – with tape –"

Leonie took them out. The old hands groped blindly for them, missed them and they fell to the ground. As Leonie picked them up, she was aware that a telephone bell which had been ringing through the house was suddenly silent. Fran, having rung off, ringing up again and receiving no answer? But Leonie had no time for telephones! The change in her grandmother frightened her.

Boadicea came up the stairs, walked in and saw Venetia.

"Law M's Sarat! Oh *my!*"

"Get her pills from her handbag and some water, quick."

"De telephone receiver were off, M's Sarat. I put it back cos there was no answer. Now it ring again. Mr. Philip am on de telephone —"

"Get him off and ring the doctor." Leonie was shaking tablets into her hand.

But when she turned to Venetia she saw that it was too late. She had had strength to tear up a sheet of the paper from the wall safe; the pieces lay scattered about her. Her head had dropped forward on to her chest, her hands were still.

Venetia Sarat was dead.

XVII

In the commotion that followed, Leonie was not aware of the sequence of things. Claire was there, and Philip and the doctor. But who came first and when they arrived, she did not know.

And then, at last, everything was quiet. An old lady was dead and there was nothing to be done — nothing except hear the truth!

Leonie was in her bedroom, fighting to collect herself, to armour herself against the shattering realisation that if she had never come to Heron House at her grandmother's invitation, no one would ever have known who killed Marcus.

She was standing by her dressing-table, staring at her reflection without seeing it, knowing that she must pull herself together and go down and join the others in the drawing-room and learn the truth from Julian. But dismay and horror and shock tore through her and there was no one to whom she could turn and say, "If I'd had any idea, I would never have started this! I'd have pushed the ghosts back into their own lost world. Only I didn't know – I couldn't guess – how *could* I?"

But there was no shoulder she could lean against and weep on; not one that could be warmly and exclusively hers.

"Leonie!"

The voice spoke her name three times before she could rouse herself to look round and see who stood at the half-open door.

Fran entered, her face white and shocked.

"I've heard – Julian told me just now! Oh, Leonie – how terrible!"

"You were on the telephone," Leonie said dully. "And Hilda came out to fetch Grandmother because you wanted to speak to her. And then – we forgot – all about you –"

"I hung on for ages and I heard running footsteps. I had a feeling something was wrong, that's why I rang off and came round." She walked to the window, staring into the darkness, and said quietly, "It's best the way it is – deep down I know it! If she'd lived, what could we have done? Kept silent – and always had that awful secret between us? We could never have told the police, could we? Not about our own grandmother!"

"No."

Fran swung round. "I'm probably going to

shock you, Leonie, but it's a release! For me, I mean! It's like being able to breathe again —"

"Because of Jim?"

"You guessed, didn't you, that I had a dreadful fear at the back of my mind I didn't dare talk about, even to myself!"

"That it might have been Jim —"

"No! Oh no! Never that! But you see, he *was* here that night! He told the truth that he'd been at Kew working in one of the glass-houses. But he came home early because he wanted to have it out once and for all with Marcus — he'd been on the telephone to me, mocking and being so cruel — you know how clever he was at hurting! There'd been that quarrel a few days earlier. Jim was talking about leaving; I begged him to stay and Marcus didn't want to lose a very fine gardener. But Marcus couldn't leave us alone; he had to telephone me and taunt me again about Jim. I shouldn't have rung Jim and told him, but I did — I was so upset. Jim left Kew about five o'clock that evening intending to have it out with Marcus and give in his notice. When he got to the house he heard voices, yours and a strange man's and there was a car in the drive. He guessed Marcus had visitors so he went away, back to Kew to vent his anger in hard work. He had no idea Marcus was dead. I believed him, Leonie. But I knew that because of that first row he'd told the police about, *they* wouldn't believe him. That's why I made him promise to tell no one about that visit the night Marcus died."

"And so you were terrified that the case might be reopened."

Fran nodded. Outside, they heard Julian calling them. Leonie took Fran's hand.

Hilda and Julian were in the drawing-room. Where Claire was, Leonie did not know. Nobody asked. Philip entered and sat quietly by the door, but Leonie's eyes didn't meet his.

Julian began without preamble. "You've heard that Venetia wanted this house and that Marcus refused to move out? When she came that night to see him, Hilda and I stayed in the car. She was gone a long time so I went to look for her. I heard angry voices; then Marcus began to play the piano — that theme music, Leonie. He played it over and over so that it burned in my mind. First he played softly, then loudly, drowning Venetia's voice, as though in defiance, to indicate that the interview with Venetia was at an end. I was at the garden door when — it happened."

"What?" she asked when he stopped talking. "What, Julian?"

"Venetia became angry. She flew at Marcus

and picked up that small stone cat that stood at his desk and threw it at him. It was an unintentionally deadly aim. Marcus fell and hit his head against the piano. That was when we heard someone in the drive – I think it must have been you, Leonie. We thought at the time it was the woman we had seen running away from the house when we arrived. Venetia and I both panicked. We fled. We knew that whoever was coming towards the house would find him and get a doctor. We didn't know until we got back to the States that Marcus had died."

"And you did nothing –"

"Venetia held a threat over me! All right, Leonie, I am a coward, but she made me one. She was strong and she had frightened me ever since I was a child; she expected so much of me – and I disappointed her. So it was easy to force my silence. After all, it was done! Marcus was dead and it was an accident."

"But Hilda must have known –"

Hilda leaned forward. "I didn't. When they got back to the car they were just very silent – they never told me anything about what had happened!"

"When we were free of the house, Venetia got control of herself. She said, as we went through the gate back to the car, 'Don't dare tell anyone — not even Hilda.' And I didn't. I knew what she meant — Hilda would have panicked and given us away by her own fright."

"And when we were back in New Orleans and I heard, I thought Julian had done it. That's why when we came here to live, I was so afraid —" Hilda cried. "I thought that Julian had — had lost his head on that awful night here. But I didn't dare ask; I was too afraid! Oh Julian," her voice broke. "I'm sorry —"

"But how *could* Grandmother have come back here to live?" Leonie demanded. "I just don't understand —"

"Venetia had no conscience, Leonie. She had been spoilt all her life; she was a law unto herself, like Marcus. Her argument was that Marcus died because he was unscrupulous, because he was trying to cheat her out of her own house. She never really blamed herself for what happened, and so she could bear to come back here and live. The only thing she seemed to be hesitating to do was to open the music-room. But she'd have got around to it without a qualm in the end. I was the squeamish one. But she made me come and she forced my silence. You see, she had made two wills, one leaving me her American holdings, and one disinheriting me. If I did what she told me, then I'd be all right for life. She was old, Leonie, she had angina. So I did what she wanted, thinking that it wouldn't be for long. Then I'd go back to the States."

"The police never saw those press-cutting books," Leonie said, thoughtfully. "Of course, they weren't here until Grandmother came over and took possession of the house —"

"That car was her love and her pride," Julian said. "She clung to it because it was the reflection of her past. She never minded if people smiled at her sitting up in it like an old queen. She only got rid of it when we came over here."

"And you couldn't have persuaded her to go to the police? After all, it was an accident!"

"An old woman of eighty-one? To expect her to face all that? And a woman like Venetia who all her life had had praise and admiration and glory? To have come back to England where she had been so great, planning to live here among that wonderful past? And then to find herself at the end of her life, standing in the dock accused of murder — or at best, manslaughter? *Of course* she ran away!"

"And the paper she destroyed?"

"Instructions to her solicitors. A or B? The one leaving me her American holdings, or the other disinheriting me," he looked across at

Philip. "You have the paper that's intact. I suppose you couldn't tell me —?"

Philip shook his head. "Not yet," he said. "I don't even know myself. The paper refers to the will that's in the office safe."

Hilda said quickly. "Does it matter? Does anything matter any more? We're free now of fear —" her hand went out to Julian.

Philip rose. "Leonie —" he said quietly and went to the door.

She got up and followed him out of the room, walking downstairs with him, a cold fear in her heart. One thought separated itself from all the rest. Philip had come in with Claire and that meant they were still together . . . and *that* meant . . . it was all over . . . and the love and hope. . . .

Philip switched on the light in the little room off the hall. Yellow brocade glowed, blue flowers bloomed in a crystal bowl.

And then Philip's arms went round her.

"Leonie!"

"Oh Philip, what happened? When you didn't come near me I was so afraid —" In that moment she knew she felt as Hilda had done, over-flowing with relief after a terrible doubt.

"There was something to be done, Leonie, before I saw you again. Something very important."

"I beg your pardon!" Claire's voice cut through the room.

She was standing in the doorway watching them without blinking, her eyes burning in her pale face.

"So this is where you got to, Philip! So much for a private talk with Julian! Or is the family conference now over and Leonie is merely consoling you until I come?"

Leonie tried to drag herself away but Philip's arm held her.

Claire limped across the room and faced them.

"Have you forgotten our conversation, Leonie? Our rather vital conversation?"

"No —"

"Then you must like playing with fire!"

"Claire," Philip's voice rapped out, "I want to have a talk with you."

"Go on, then."

"I would prefer it if we were alone."

"I'll go," Leonie said quickly.

"No, don't," Claire spoke. "You stay and listen to what I've got to say to Philip!"

"But do you want Leonie to hear what *I've* got to say to *you?"* he asked quietly.

She laughed at them both. "When I've finished talking I don't think either of you will have much to say." She perched herself on the

287

edge of the table. "This is going to be interesting! Shall I start?"

"No, I will," Philip said unexpectedly. "Claire, why did you send Leonie an anonymous letter?"

Leonie murmured: "Claire!" But Philip laid a detaining hand on her arm; his eyes didn't move from Claire's face.

"It would be interesting to know what you're talking about."

"You know — and I know that you do!"

"Have you taken leave of your senses? What sort of letter am I supposed to have written? And in heaven's name, why?"

"I'll tell you the sort of letter and then *you* tell me why you did it. It threatened a whispering campaign against Leonie, hinting that she knew more about Marcus's murder than she had told. It ordered her to leave Heron House."

"Why should I write such a letter? I'm not afraid of Leonie. And I should be very careful if I were you, Philip, about accusations of this kind. You should know the law too well to run risks of an action for slander."

"These past few days I've been working on a hunch about that letter."

"Then why don't you go to the police?" she countered.

"I intend to —"

A quiver ran through Claire. She dropped her eyes, but she was still smiling that curious smile without pleasure.

"My hunch led me to Swanwell. You know, Claire, the place where you are working on Julia Mandeley's house. I went to the offices of the local paper and looked up some back copies, ones prior to the sending of that note. You see, it was composed of letters cut out of a newspaper. But you know that, don't you?"

"No. Never mind, *do* go on!" Her fingers held tightly to the edge of the table.

"I found a newspaper dated twenty-fourth May. In it was half a column about the house you and de Crispin were working on. I guessed you'd have a copy of that for your publicity file. So I studied every page. On the note Leonie received were two words not made out of separate letters but with the whole word cut out. One word was "Career," and the other was "Campaign." And both these words were contained in headlines in the newspaper. The type was identical. The only person, Claire, who could have had reason to have that newspaper and to know Leonie, was you."

Claire slid off the table. Her body was like a coiled spring. Only the hands showed her emotions; they flexed and tensed, working like cats' claws.

"And suppose what you say is true," her voice mocked. "You wouldn't go to the police with that story! You see, I would have to explain in court why I did such a desperate thing. That I lost my head and was beside myself with grief because a man I loved, and for whom I had gone through so much, was being taken from me by — an actress." She made it sound evil.

"By all means go to court!" Philip's voice was calm and cold. "I'll fight. But the really dangerous statement in your letter seems to have escaped you. You hint that Leonie knew far more than she ever told about Marcus's death — you're almost hinting at her guilt. That is a point at issue in that letter — the point the police would be most interested in," he looked at her with pity. "Oh Claire, why were you never honest with me?"

"I don't know what you mean!" She managed to look bewildered, but her eyes were bold and watchful.

"About Marcus," Philip said patiently. "You knew him very well, didn't you? Well enough, in fact to visit him without anyone knowing, because you knew your father hated him. He couldn't refuse the Sarat business, but he never trusted Marcus and so, while he was alive, you never dared let him know you were seeing Marcus. And then he was killed and soon after that your father died. By that time there was an understanding between you and me."

"You have far too much imagination for a lawyer, Philip!" she said with a little sneer.

"No, Claire, none of this is imagination. Venetia found out."

"An old woman cooking up some story —"

"She was troubled about the fact that you seemed to know the house very well. She spoke to me about it, but I had no idea that you knew Marcus. You saw him on the night of his death, didn't you?" His eyes were stern and steady and unrelenting.

Claire was strong, but not strong enough to withstand Philip's barrage. Defiance dropped visibly from her. Anger took over. She was shaking and her eyes blazed. Her quiet, little-girl voice changed, she almost screamed at him.

"All right, so I knew Marcus! I did! I loved him. Did you hear what I said? *I loved him!* And then that old woman killed him. Oh I know she did; you told me to make myself scarce as there was a family conference, but I listened at the door. I heard what Julian said. *She* killed him — and when he died, nothing mattered for me any more." Her voice broke and then became strong again as though she despised weakness. "Immediately after Marcus was killed, you came along — someone who didn't mind being seen with me with my hideous leg —"

"You make too much of your lameness, Claire," he said quietly. "Yours is only temporary, and some people go through all their lives with handicaps and manage to be loved very much. After all, it doesn't seem that Marcus minded!"

"He *loathed* it!" she said with hissing violence. "Even if he had lived until after my father had died, he would never have taken me around with him until after the operation. I understood because I hated it, too. Marcus wasn't kind about it —"

"And yet you loved him —"

Claire was shaking. "And this talk about love! What do you know of it? You — or Leonie? But *I* do! I loved Marcus more than any other man I shall ever meet. He was malicious and cruel, but he was brilliant and exciting!" She broke off and her eyes looked away beyond the room. "I gave Marcus that little cat. . . . He thought it so beautiful — but it killed him. Don't look at me like that!" She swung round. "If you had never come here, " she flung at Leonie, "no one would ever have known who killed Marcus or − about Marcus and me." Her eyes narrowed. "The Sarat family; I'm sick of them − I'm sick of you all. Oh, go to the devil!" She turned and stumbled from the room.

Leonie listened to her limping footsteps going up the stairs.

"What shall we do about her, Philip?"

"Leave her. She'll pack her things and go."

"*I* want to get away, too! I don't want to sleep in this house to-night."

"You shan't. I'll take you back to your flat."

"I'd like to slip away without seeing Julian or Hilda −"

"That's all right. There's nothing for you to do here. I'll explain to them while you pack."

"Tell them − I'll come and see them in a few days −"

"Of course. Go, Leonie. I'll be waiting for you in the garden."

"Philip, did you agree to bribe Johnnie to keep away from Claire?"

"Good heavens, no!"

"And another thing −" she hesitated. "What made you think that Claire might have sent that letter?"

"It occurred to me when I left you that night and you told me she had threatened to take me to court. I thought, if she could dare to stand in the witness box and lie, a little thing like an anonymous letter wouldn't worry her in the least. The question was, why did she send it?"

"Exactly. She had everything she wanted – or so we thought."

"She had been tossing out little barbed thrusts about you in her conversation. It made me realise that there was something she had against you –" He broke off. "Let's leave it at that, Leonie, shall we?" He gave her a gentle push. "Go and pack! *Go,* my darling!"

When she had finished, she took her two suitcases into the hall. Then she went to find Boadicea. She was sitting on the floor, outside the dead Venetia's room.

Gently Leonie helped the ungainly figure to her feet: she said softly,

"Grandmother was very old and I can't explain things to you now, but what's happened is for the best."

"I bin with her, M's Sarat, for fifteen years!"

"Will you stay here for the next few weeks, Boadicea? Mr. Julian and Mrs. Hilda will be remaining here for the time being, and I want you to think very carefully what you want to do. Don't make any decisions now, wait till the shock is over, then, if you want to return to New Orleans, I'll see that you get there. Mr. Julian may eventually go back, but, if he doesn't offer you a job with him, will you consider working for us – Mr. Drew and I?"

"You, M's Sarat and Mr. *Drew?*" A faint puzzled smile touched the stark misery of her face. "Oh lor! Oh lor' me!"

Leonie knew she was wondering about Claire, but too shy and much too conscious of her position to ask about her.

"Go and make yourself a cup of tea," Leonie said kindly. "You can do nothing here."

"M's Sarat –"

Leonie had been walking away. She turned and waited.

"I sur' would like workin' for you, M's Sarat!"

"Good! Then we'll talk about it later. And, Boadicea, don't fret too much."

She left her going slowly down the back staircase to her colourful kitchen, and went to find Philip.

Before she reached the front door of the house, however, Hilda came down the stairs.

She roamed round the hall, touching the flowers, touching a large vellum-bound book Julian had brought home.

"I've been in pretty good hell, Leonie, thinking it was Julian!" She looked up. "Can you imagine what it's like to suspect your own husband? It's quite horrible –"

"And all this time, you never talked to him about it!"

"No! When I was in New Orleans I could try and forget it. Here, it was everywhere, shrieking at me from the walls. And I daren't say anything! I wonder how many wives would? They might say: 'Oh, of course I'd ask him, I'd *have* to know!' But they wouldn't! They'd be like I was, afraid of knowing the truth that he had killed a man or, being even more afraid that, if he thought I suspected, I'd be in danger! People aren't nearly as brave with their husbands as they like outsiders to think." She turned away from the table. "And now it's all over. Leonie, can you believe even now that Venetia did that — that awful thing and then chose to come back here and live?"

"Yes," Leonie said. "I can. She had argued to herself that it was an accident, that Marcus goaded her. I think she'd learned to dismiss the past; to live in the present. Only, things that happened in the house wouldn't let her; things she hadn't bargained for. And she found herself caught up in it all again, not quite knowing who it was who had run from the house in the darkness and who might have come back — to find Marcus dead. She realised then that someone could have heard her coming towards the house and stopped in the dark garden and watched. So, she was never quite certain whether whoever had been there had seen her or not."

"And even *that* didn't make her pack up and leave?"

"Do you really think my grandmother would run away? She was wild and temperamental and self-willed, but she was no coward!"

"And now," Hilda said again, as though she could still scarcely believe it, "it's all over. Oh Leonie – I know Venetia is dead, but it means we can live our own lives at last!"

Leonie looked up and round the great hall. The house, she thought, the house too, is breathing again, emerging from its great cloud into the light. The beautiful, gracious house that had the stone heron to guard it.

She said, "I'm going out for a while to talk to Philip and then I'm going back to my flat. You understand, don't you?"

"I expected you'd go," Hilda said. "I should think you'd want to get free of this house –"

"Only for a while."

"You'll come and see us sometime while we're still in England?"

"Of course. But you may go back to the States."

"I hope we do – oh I do hope so! You see, it's our country, Leonie, just as this is yours.

But we'll have to stay for some time while Julian clears up Venetia's affairs."

"If you or Julian want me, you know my address."

"Yes!"

"Good-bye Hilda."

She felt that Hilda was glad she was going, as though she were the last danger in the house. And then remembered that Hilda didn't know yet that she loved Philip and would marry him. She went out into the warm night and found Philip at the terrace-edge. In the distance, the moonlight glimmered on to the Thames. There was a hint of a breeze coming from the west.

They stood together without touching one another. They were both spent with their emotion and the shock of the night, and yet, through it, the aftermath of peace was stealing over them.

"Philip." Leonie broke the quiet. "Nobody will ever need to know, will they, about Grandmother. Nobody but just us few, I mean?"

"No."

"Claire might tell. She said she listened at the door."

"Claire won't dare tell anything. She withheld evidence from the police, remember."

So still, in the eyes of the world, she would

be Venetia Sarat, one of the greatest actresses of her day. The face that enchanted; the voice that enthralled – but a woman without a conscience, without a heart, she who could stir millions to tears. . . .

"Philip –"

"Now what?" His hand touched her cheek.

"I have a career, too! But I'll give it up if you want me to."

His arm drew her close. "My darling, you shall do that in your own time. At least, though, just for a little I want to bask in reflected glory – to be able to say to the world: 'Leonie Sarat? Why, she's my wife!' " His lips touched hers. They said: "and my love. . . ."

THORNDIKE PRESS HOPES you
have enjoyed this Large Print
book. All our Large Print titles
are designed for the easiest
reading, and all our books are
made to last. Other Thorndike
Press Large Print books are
available at your library,
through selected bookstores, or
directly from the publisher. For
more information about our
current and upcoming Large
Print titles, please send your
name and address to:

THORNDIKE PRESS
ONE MILE ROAD
P.O. Box 157
THORNDIKE, MAINE 04986

There is no obligation, of course.